ANGRY GIRL

A FANTASY ADVENTURE

THE CRIMSHADE CHRONICLES
BOOK ONE

MARY E. TWOMEY

MARY E. TWOMEY, LLC

ANGRY GIRL

Book One in the Crimshade Chronicles

By

Mary E. Twomey

COPYRIGHT

DEDICATION

To Sunday

Who taught me more than I ever dreamed I would need to know about compassion.

NEW PET

*L*aundry. Dishes. Change bedding. Vacuum.

My list flicks over my brain as if that will open a time-space continuum in which any of those tasks will be possible to do in the twenty minutes before I need to pick up Seven from school.

No calls home from the principal today. That's good.

I really thought being an aunt would be more fun than this, but when my sister died three years ago, I inherited all her junk and the cutest kid in the world.

Got rid of the junk. Kept the kid.

Laundry. Dishes. Change bedding. Vacuum.

I check my phone under my desk, grateful my boss isn't doing one of his patrols to check that we're all "doing our best work."

It's an internet call center. We're all just trying to make it through the day with our self-esteem intact. Being yelled at over and over because of router or modem issues wasn't what I'd hoped my high school diploma would get me, but it pays the bills, which have skyrocketed with the introduction of my seven-year-old cutie.

No messages from the teacher. That's good.

Eleven messages from Jonathan, which is nothing new or urgent.

He had a date last night with someone he clicked with on the dating app he loves. The plan was to take the guy out on the three Ds: dinner, drinks and dancing. That's his standard when testing out a new guy to see if he can become the new boyfriend-for-two-weeks.

It's when I have zero messages from Jonathan that I worry.

Eleven means they had the three Ds and it went fine. Possibly four, if all went well. No bail or wedding bells needed.

I return my focus to my work screen, sighing before I click to connect to the next caller.

No greeting, no pauses, just ranting, as per usual.

"This stupid piece of crap isn't working! I pay good money to..."

I tug the headset off for a solid half a minute, which is how long these rants typically last.

For my last call of the day, I'm hoping to wrap this one up quick, so I can at least throw a load of laundry in the wash before I pick up Seven and her friend at the bus stop.

I pack up my purse, tossing the wrapper from my sad

snack of seasoned nuts that tasted too stale to be called a treat.

I down the last of my water and locate my keys, so I can sprint out as soon as the clock releases me from call center purgatory.

I place my headset back on just as the man finishes his rant. "I'm happy to send someone out to you first thing tomorrow."

It's never first thing, but that's the script we're told to follow. Calms the customer for the moment and gives them a false hope that help is promptly on the way, which it most certainly is not.

I schedule the service visit, end the call, and punch out, but cringe when my boss' voice hits my ears.

"Sara, come here for a second. There's someone I want you to meet."

My lips press in a tight line as I direct my feet to move to my boss' office, where I see two white men in suits. "What can I do for you, Mister Jones? I was just on my way out."

His smile is jovial, and his eyes are wide, which means he is trying to impress these two men. "I was just telling our colleagues from corporate about our diversity program." He turns to them. "See? Sara is from India."

My stomach churns and my attitude flares. "My name is Zara, actually." It's only the fifteenth time I've corrected him. "My grandfather immigrated from India. I'm from Ohio."

I will not be their token brown person so they can check some diversity box and pat themselves on the back for a job not even half done.

The men smile and nod as if I haven't spoken. As if I'm some oddity for which they can take credit.

Whatever. I don't have time for this.

Laundry. Dishes. Change bedding. Vacuum.

I spin on my heel and march out, gritting my teeth to keep from spewing out that I am the only person of color on the floor.

It's not worth the argument. It never is.

And so my current of anger slowly boils until one day, I inevitably bubble over. Then I'll be labeled the angry girl.

Super.

The sunshine sparkling off the snowdrifts doesn't even brighten my mood as I tug my long, black hair into a high ponytail.

I take a cleansing breath because if I don't, I imagine fire might come shooting out of me if one more person calls me Sara.

I take in another deep, cleansing breath on my way to my green sedan, bumping the side with my hip because otherwise the driver's side door doesn't open.

On my third breath, I have officially left behind the more arduous aspects of the office. It's amazing what a few deep breaths can do to cleanse out the poison that threatens to set in deep.

Laundry. Dishes. Change bedding. Vacuum.

I turn onto the main road, driving through what was ice and snow this morning, but is now salted and sludgy. As my tires are bald and have zero traction, if I take a turn too quickly, I start to feel like I'm driving a motorized roller skate on an ice rink.

Laundry. Dishes. Change bedding. Vacuum.

I'm going to make it home with twenty minutes to spare if I don't hit the usual traffic.

By the time I pull into my condo, I have nineteen minutes to complete my chores, so I dash into the house and collect all the dirty clothes and sheets in the house, shoving them into the washing machine that practically groans at being overfilled. I grimace as I tug out a few of Seven's dresses that she has reminded me over and over need to be handwashed.

Did I put laundry detergent in before I turned it on?

I freeze, trying to recall my actions, and finally decide to hope for the best.

New sheets are shoved on the two mattresses, and I make sure Seven's bed is made nicely, with all of her plushies and pillows arranged just how she likes them.

The dishes aren't piled high, but yesterday's dinner was an event with four courses, so a little elbow grease is necessary.

I mull over the things I need to do still, watching the time out of the corner of my eye while I scrub the tomato cream sauce out of the pot.

The clock is yellow and purple with a brown elephant in the center. It was my mother's, and her mother's before that. The ticking of the purple pendulum serves as a constant reminder that I need to hurry, because no matter how focused I stay, I am always running behind while the tasks pile up.

When my time is up, the dishes are mostly done.

No time to vacuum.

I really want this play date to go well. Seven's been reminding me every day for the past week that Addison is coming over.

No matter how many times I invite a child over via their parent, they've all politely declined. I like to pretend people are just busy, but I know that Seven being born a boy and identifying as a girl has their heads spinning.

No, you can't catch transgender.

No, my sister wasn't a permissive parent who somehow failed.

No, your child won't suddenly decide to forsake their assigned-at-birth gender just because they play with Seven.

I have been working hard on greasing the wheels with Addison's mother, and finally, we have a playdate.

I shove my running shoes back on and dash out the front door, winded smile in place.

Today is the big day, and the house is pretty well cleaned.

Except I forgot to vacuum.

I wince at the oversight before the voice of reason taps me on the shoulder. Seven-year-olds don't care if it's been two days since I've vacuumed.

In fact, seven-year-olds don't care that Seven is transgender. They just want to play on the swings, go on the monkey bars, and play tag—all things Seven can do.

I shove my arms through my red winter jacket, throwing it over my plain black t-shirt and jeans—a look I haven't felt a need to venture away from ever in my life.

I do my best run-walk to the bus stop.

I beat the bus by ten whole seconds, my smile fading when I catch sight of Addison's mom. "Hi, Julie. Everything okay? I thought I was picking up the girls for the playdate."

Julie dons a bright smile, her head tilted to the side. "Bad news! Addison can't come over today. I forgot we had a thing."

My entire demeanor crashes, the world dimming because it has become predictable. "That's a shame. Seven was really looking forward to it."

Julie bats off my concern. "Oh, they can see each other in school."

"Another time, then?"

Julie shrugs noncommittally. "Maybe." Then she turns her back on me, waving to Addison, who steps off the bus.

I don't know why I got my hopes up.

But I'm not the only crushed girl, it seems. When Seven steps off the bus, her shoulders are drooped and there is red around her eyes. She insisted her raven hair be twisted into two high buns atop her head, showing off her long eyelashes and the prettiest smile that ever was. Seven had me take off her nail polish this morning because she set up a manicure station in the bathroom for her and Addison to play beauty parlor.

Her teal dress sticking out from beneath her winter coat is poofy with glittery tulle, making her look like a tragic ballerina the world might never understand. Her usually chipper steps are weighted as she walks to me, slumping into my arms with the last of her ability to keep her tears at bay.

"Addison can't come over!" she wails, sniffling her sadness into my shirt.

The other parents collect their children while I get on my knees to comfort Seven. "Sometimes that happens, babe. I'm so sorry."

"Addison said her mom won't let her come over because I'm supposed to be a boy!" She motions to her outfit. "But I'm not a boy!"

I fix Julie with my most vindictive glare, glad that Addison dropped her backpack, so Julie has to pause and hear the pain she's caused my baby.

"Addison's mom will grow up one day." I watch Julie wither under the weight of Seven's heartbreak and my death stare. "Until then, we give her the space to educate herself." I hate that I have to tell Seven these things. I hate that she needs to be understanding when the adults refuse to even try their hand at empathy.

I hate that a child has to be the adult because the adults around us are constantly failing to rise to the challenge.

I want to go egg Julie's perfect BMW. I want to take a baseball bat to her stain-free windows.

There'll be plenty of time for that after Seven goes to sleep. Not now. Right now, Seven's tears are the only things that matter. Each and every one of them are mine to collect and tend to until Seven has the strength to dry them herself.

Instead, I lock eyes with Seven, making sure I am on her height level, though my knees are chilled and damp from the iced sidewalk. "You look at me, Seven. I know you're a girl because you told me that's who you are. I hear you, and it's obvious that you're a girl. Some people are just plain ignorant."

Seven sniffles and nods, which means she is putting her armor back on. She will retreat to her books, withdrawing and making herself smaller to fit in this world that dares tell her who she has to be.

As if they give a crap about her.

I take out my phone and shoot a quick text. "I'll tell you what; Papa Jonathan is going to come over instead of Addison, okay? We're going to do all the things with him that we planned to do with Addison. Nails, cookie decorating, karaoke, fashion shows. All of it."

Though Seven adores my best friend, it's not the same as a girl your own age. However, the consolation prize dries her tears enough for us to hold hands on the way home, her backpack slung over my shoulder.

Halfway home, we stop when I hear a wounded whine that sounds like it's coming from a dog in need of a vet.

Seven and I both turn toward the sound, our hearts too tender to keep walking home if an animal is hurt. Flashbacks of the two weeks spent nursing a nest of abandoned baby birds back to health hit me. I sincerely hope this animal doesn't need as much round-the-clock care as they did.

Seven squeezes my hand. "Mama, do you hear that?"

I nod as the yodeling whine grows louder. "Sounds like a dog."

Seven's footsteps carry us down a street between two fast food restaurants that sit a block from our condo complex.

It's more of an alleyway, though it's clean enough not to look too skeevy.

"Honey, we can't touch the dog if he's here. They tend to bite when they're injured." I know this from my own childhood spent begging my mom for a dog and being constantly turned down. I even wrote her a paper on all the things I knew about dogs, since my mother responded to things like good grades rather than emotion.

Still no dice.

Now I'm the adult, and I still don't have a dog, but it's

because the past three years have been a complete upheaval of everything I thought I knew.

We keep walking toward the sound because neither Seven nor I have the ability to turn off our hearts when someone is hurting. Even though her heart was just broken by bigotry, she cares more about a dog's pain than her own.

She's a classy kid, that's for certain.

I hold tight to her hand while we walk down the alley, moving toward the sad sound that is coming from the other side of the dumpster.

Seven's gasp is louder than mine. "Oh, Mommy! He's hurt! His leg is bleeding!"

Sure enough, a huge dog is sitting in the dirty snow, whining while he licks his bloody leg. I've never been near all that many dogs in my life, but this one looks, I don't know, forlorn somehow. His long maw doesn't jerk up at us as if he wants to guard himself or warn us away. He looks defeated.

Just like us.

Seven tugs on my arm. "Mommy, he doesn't have a collar. No one is coming for him." She feigns a dramatic shiver. "It's so cold out. We can't just leave him here!"

I pinch the bridge of my nose, sounding exactly like my mom, which I really never saw coming. "He's a wild animal, Sev. Wounded, wild animals tend to attack people even if they have good intentions."

Seven's lower lip quivers. "Then can I sleep out here

with him tonight? If he can't come home with us, I'll bring my sleeping bag out here to make sure he's okay." Her hand moves over her heart in a swoon directed at the dog. "Oh, baby!"

In her tender plea, I see my little girl self, begging my mom to let me have a dog of my very own.

I swallow several curse words that I had to give up when I welcomed Seven into my home three years ago, back when she identified as a little girl named Four.

"You're not sleeping in the snow, babe. Back up." I am such a sucker for this kid. She never asks for anything self-ish, so it's hard to say no to her sweet nature.

Seven obeys, dropping my hand and stepping back, her palm over her mouth while I fix the huge dog with my most intimidating glare. As if the dog can understand me, I hold my finger out to scold it. "If you can't walk, I'm going to have to pick you up. Got it? I'm going to take you home so I can call Animal Control. Then they'll take it from there."

The dog lowers its maw, as if willing to accept my terms. Or maybe it's gearing up to bite me. I have no idea.

I keep my stern finger aloft. "If you bite me, I will drop you on your furry butt. Got it?"

Again, the dog acts as if it understands me, granting me a whine so pathetic, my heart nearly turns into the same puddle of goo as Seven's.

A deep breath fills my lungs as I steady myself before doing the thing common sense warns me not to try.

But I've got a child watching me, and an unrequited love for dogs inside my heart, so I put on my brave face and lean down, grunting at the effort involved in lifting what feels like an elephant but looks like an overgrown brown and gray dog.

"Oof!" I nearly buckle under his weight, but thankfully, he doesn't make a move to bite me.

Seven runs to my side, fawning over his wounded leg. She squeals with trepidation, standing on her toes at the prospect of me bringing home a dog—a thing I firmly told us both I would not do. I don't have time to take care of a pet. Especially not one this big. It's not a Newfoundland, but just as giant as one. It looks like a wolf mixed with… I dunno. Some sort of really hairy breed.

This seems like a good compromise. She gets a dog for a few hours until Animal Control comes by to collect him.

As soon as the dog rests his body against my chest, his massive maw on my shoulder, I swear, I feel him say, *"Thanks."* It's not out loud, and there's no one around for their voice to carry into the alley, but I hear it as much as I feel it vibrate through my body.

"You're welcome," I grumble, pretending it's the dog who is grateful. "If you pee on my carpet, I will throw you out into the snow. Got it?"

"Hungry," the voice says again.

I freeze, knowing the first time I could have been mistaken, but that time I definitely heard something.

"He's hungry, Mommy!" Seven frets.

Ice zips through my veins. "Did you hear that?"

Seven nods, as if a dog communicating in a human voice without the effort of even openings its mouth is nothing abnormal. Her tone turns syrupy. "Do you want some chicken? We made murgh makhani last night. It's yummy-yummy." She runs her hand over his thick fur.

Again, I hear that same masculine voice. *"Please."*

I don't understand what's going on, but I know my fingers are starting to get chilly. "Let's go. You lead the way, Sev. This mutt is hard to see over." I lean my cheek to his. "It's okay, baby boy. We'll take care of you now."

I cringe at how fully owned I am by the sight of a wounded animal. The adult in me recoils from the added responsibility, but the child in me who never got what she wanted dances for joy.

The dog sighs in my arms, making him impossibly heavier. His weight combined with the slippery pavement is making this a horrible idea. Still, I put one foot in front of the other, following the sound of Seven's squeals as I take this smelly talking dog to our home.

SMELLY TALKING DOG

The ruined playdate with Addison is long forgotten when we cross the threshold of our condo. The clean kitchen and tidy living room seem to mock me as I bring a dirty, bleeding wet dog through the house and land in the bathroom.

I have never taken care of a wounded animal of this size before, but the bathtub seems the right place to contain this furry fellow while I gather my bearings.

I shake out my arms, breathless at the short walk that felt unbearably long when paired with carrying a huge dog that might outweigh me.

Seven flits through the house, collecting things she thinks the dog will like, including a box of her favorite glittery pink band-aids she reserves for special injuries.

At least she has a plan.

I brace myself with my hands on my knees while I catch my breath, wondering when the last time was that I exercised.

I frown at the dog while Seven runs to her bedroom, grabbing who knows what to comfort the newcomer. "Don't get any ideas," I tell the dog. "You're not staying, no matter how much Seven wants a dog. No matter how much *I* want a dog. You're going with Animal Control. That's more than anyone's done for you, so I don't want to hear any complaining."

The dog's fur is matted in parts, bloody and muddy, leaving him looking completely forlorn. He whines again, and that same unspoken male voice filters through my body. *"Hungry."*

I purse my lips, wondering if this is what extreme stress does to a person. Maybe Cinderella wasn't magical, talking to animals as she did. Maybe she just cracked under the weight of caring for a household.

I jab my finger at the dog, refusing to soften. "I'll grab you some leftovers, but don't get too comfortable."

My feet carry me to the kitchen, where the remnants of our meal are nicely stacked in containers in the fridge.

The rest of the murgh makhani was supposed to be my lunch for the week, and now it's going to a dog.

I mean, honestly.

I try to maintain my indignation, so I don't cave and turn into a puddle of snuggles and welcoming kisses. I really don't have the bandwidth to adopt a dog.

I pop open the lid, wondering if dogs are allowed to eat serrano peppers. I don't know anything about feeding an animal, so I do a quick internet search on my phone, looking up the key ingredients to make sure they're safe.

Jonathan's text dings, assuring me that he'll be by the second work ends for the day for him, armed with girl day supplies.

Thank God for my best friend.

Though, Seven is so pleased to have a dog in the house that she's completely forgotten about her devastation over Addison's cancellation.

I inhale a long, steadying breath and then move back into the bathroom, where Seven is petting the mutt atop his head.

I shriek my worry without a filter. "Sev, back up! It's a wild animal, honey. Don't pet him without me right beside you. If you were bitten, I would never forgive myself."

But even as I say this, the dog rolls over as best it can in the tub, exposing his belly for Seven to rub.

And just like that, my heart melts all over again, no matter how quickly I try to pack it in ice.

This dog, I swear.

Seven coos to the giant dog that looks crammed into the tub, its body too big for the space. "Poor baby! He would never bite me, Mommy. He loves me." She spots the dish in my hand and lights up. "Oh, good! He's been saying he's hungry. Should we warm the food up?"

I shake my head. "I don't think dogs care if food is

warm or not." I kneel beside my niece—my daughter—my movements tentative as I set the dish beside the dog's maw after he rolls back so he's upright again in the tub. I purse my lips while I study his careful movements. "I don't know if you like spice, but we do, so brace yourself if you've got a vanilla palate."

I'm talking to this dog as if he understands the nuances of my words.

I have no idea what I'm doing.

"Food," the dog sighs in the same nonverbal, verbal way. A wave of contentment fills the room, letting me know that he is happy with anything I give him—so great is his hunger.

My heart tugs in my chest.

We were never hungry—my sister and me. Our mom worked hard at two different jobs to make sure we always had food on the table. This dog doesn't have anyone looking after him.

After my mother passed, I looked after Aashya, since I'm the older sister. No one ever needed to look after me from the time I hit puberty on. My mom had enough on her plate without worrying about laundry and whatnot. So, I took care of Aashya.

Now I look after Seven.

And this smelly dog.

While I want to remain stalwartly stoic toward this dog, watching him eat while Seven pets his head does something to my heart I was not expecting.

I don't have time to look after a dog. I still haven't vacuumed the house yet. I have enough on my plate, navigating the ins and outs of raising an orphaned child.

The dog whines, leaning into Seven's palm.

Seven coos, leaning forward to kiss his head. "My baby-baby."

"Stop!" I warn her. "This dog is filthy. Don't kiss him."

Seven frowns at the muddy, matted fur. "Good thing he's in the bathtub."

I don't understand what she means until she removes the licked clean dish and turns on the water, testing the temperature with her little hand. "Don't worry, baby-baby," she coos at him. "The water will heat up in a few seconds. Do you want bubbles? Bubble baths are the best. You deserve a nice, relaxing bubble bath."

I groan aloud, my eyes closing to pray for patience. "Okay, hun. Don't plug up the drain. We have to wash this mud off first, otherwise he'll be soaking in filthy water. He's got an injury too, so let me handle that part."

Seven nods happily. "Smart thinking." She tilts her head to the side while she adjusts the water's temperature, noting the dog's tail flicking at the feel of chilly water on his hind quarters. "What should we call him?"

"We can't name him, honey. It'll just make it harder when Animal Control comes. Remember, we aren't keeping him. We're just giving him a meal and a bath, and then he's going with the city. They'll find him a home."

Or, more likely, they'll have to put him down after a month of no one adopting a dog as big as a recliner.

But I don't mention that, so I don't break Seven's little heart, or my own. Picturing this sweet mountain of a mutt in a cold cell of the animal shelter is more than I can stand. I open my mouth to tell her he can stay the night, but then snap it shut, remembering that this is simply not something I have the bandwidth to do.

Seven grabs for the shampoo and squeezes a dollop into her palm. "What should we call you? Bernie? I like Bernie. Like Bert and Ernie. Bernie."

"Connery," the voice informs us in a raggedy cadence. *"Connery Alpin. But I'll be Bernie, if ye prefer."*

I've never met anyone with that name before, so I know it didn't come from my brain.

Seven lights up. "I like the name Connery. So cool. Like a movie hero."

Goosebumps blister out over my skin as I sit back on my heels. "Where did you hear that name? Do you have a friend at school called Connery?"

Please say there is a kid at school named Connery. Please tell me we both didn't just hear the same voice that clearly isn't speaking aloud.

Seven shrugs, scrubbing the shampoo over Connery's tail. "He told me that's his name. I think it's nice." She looks up at me with hope blooming in her big brown eyes. "Mommy, we were meant to be. I understand him perfectly. He needs us." Then she indulges in a round of baby talk while I fend off a panic attack. She does the dirty work, for the most part, until her hands reach his front paws.

It's then that I push aside my existential crisis and reach for the shampoo. "I'll do the rest, Sev. Dogs don't like it when you touch their wounded paw. I don't want him to bite you."

I stand up and grab the shower attachment, turning that on so I can scrub down his head and paws. This bathroom was completely scrubbed clean last night, the light-blue tile gleaming against the cream-colored floor. Now it's covered in dog hair, mud, and blood.

And yet I cannot stop my heart from softening, from gathering up his fur in my hands and making an adorable mohawk just to make Seven giggle. I kiss his soapy face, scrubbing away a portion of his sadness as best I can.

It takes us the better part of an hour to get this dog fed and cleaned, but after the water finally runs clear, I can see that the raw injury on his front leg seems to have clotted, thank goodness. It still looks dreadful, with the fur gone and the skin most certainly infected.

He doesn't even shake the water droplets from his fur but lays patiently while Seven and I rub his body with all the clean towels in the house.

"*Thirsty,*" comes the voice again.

"Stop that!" I snap at him, more than a little spooked at the sound. "You're talking, but that's not possible."

Seven shoots me a scolding look. "If you don't get him a bowl of water, I will."

Dread sinks in my bones again. "You heard him say that?"

She nods, as if nothing unusual at all just happened. "Connery is thirsty."

"He was just surrounded by water!"

Seven makes a face. "Dirty, soapy, bloody water. He shouldn't have to drink that. He's a guest in our home. He can have clean water."

"Okay, babe. I'll get Connery some water." Anxiety runs through me as I move into the kitchen to fill my salad bowl with clean water.

When I come back. Connery is out of the tub, sitting like a good boy at Seven's side while she wraps her arms around his middle, snuggling into his thick, clean gray and brown fur.

"Thirsty. Please," the dog says without moving his maw.

With tentative steps and a cautious gaze, I set the bowl of water on the cream-colored tile, swallowing hard as the dog laps up the liquid.

I wonder when the last time was that he had something clean to drink.

Before I can talk sense into my brain, my hand reaches down to brush through his fur.

I can see that he's not putting any weight on his injured front right paw while he drinks. That can't be good.

"Seven, get my first aid kit. It's just under the sink there."

She holds up her glittery band-aids. "Will these work?"

An indulgent smile crosses my features. "No, they'll get stuck in his fur. He needs that leg wrapped until he can go to the doggy doctor. I have an extra bandage in there."

I have an extra everything in that first aid kit. The second I brought Seven into my home, I pretty much bought out the first aid supplies for every possible scenario, just in case.

The only thing I didn't buy was the glittery band-aids, which turned out to be the one thing Seven goes through like water.

Connery's voice comes out in a humble, hollow sound, his head dipping low. *"You're helping me. Why?"*

I tilt my head to the side. "You're in pain. Of course we're going to help you. Drink up, babe."

Connery shies away from the bowl, though I know he's still thirsty. *"I don't want to take the last of your water. Ye have a wee one to take care of."*

I purse my lips. "There's no shortage of water here. Drink that, and I'll get you more. As much as you like, and I promise it won't take away from Seven getting all the water she needs."

Connery's movements are hesitant, but he decides to take me at my word and laps up the liquid.

I run my fingers over his thick fur while he drinks his fill. "How did you injure yourself?"

His head sinks lower, and when he speaks again, I pick out an Irish or Scottish brogue. *"Ye wouldn't help me if ye knew."*

My lips purse before I argue. With a talking dog. I run my fingers through his clean fur, then bring his maw up to kiss it. "Your only job is to let us be good to you. That's your full-time job for the next..." I want to say he'll only be here another hour or two, but maybe he should stay the night. I don't want him putting pressure on his bad leg.

Seven scoots out of the way, snuggling on the other side of the dog, petting him while he drinks. "We won't let you out of our sight, baby-baby," she coos. "Everything's going to be okay now."

I occupy myself with trying to figure out if some sort of deep cleaning spray or cream should be used on the dog before I bandage his arm up.

"I have no idea what I'm doing," I warn them both. "Can I use this spray antibacterial stuff on a dog?" I mutter while reading the label's instructions.

"Same stuff you'd use on a human will work on me," Connery tells me as he laps up the water.

The complete sentence spooks me anew, but I muscle through my panic and shake the spray, in case that's a thing I should be doing.

"This is going to sting," I warn him.

Seven squeaks her nerves, her arms wrapping around Connery to brace him for the discomfort. "It's going to be okay! It's going to be okay! Be brave, baby Connery!"

Even I wince as I spray the area. It's hard to tell what caused the injury, but it looks like the fur and skin have been shredded in parts, exposing the raw pink beneath.

Connery leans into Seven's comfort, pausing his drinking while the sting settles in and does what disinfecting spray is supposed to do.

"I'm sorry!" I yelp when Connery sighs. Though, I can't tell if he's uncomfortable, or if he just loves being consoled so wholeheartedly by Seven's unrelenting embrace.

A quiet chuckle comes from him as he licks Seven's cheek. *"I'm grand,"* he assures us, even though I know that spray stings.

My fingers fumble with the bandage as I wrap it around and around, dropping the thing several times and adjusting the tension, making it abundantly clear that I have no idea what I'm doing.

When I finish, my chest shudders with worry. I lean back, my spine to the tub, my clothes soaked and muddied, and my energy completely spent. "There," I tell them both, breathless. "He's cleaned, fed, watered and bandaged." Instead of opting for denial, relying on common sense instead of questioning the oddity of a dog talking in plain English. I lock eyes with Connery. "Is there anything else you need?"

Connery licks Seven's hand and then breaks gently from her embrace to swing his head closer to me. He licks my knuckle and then cranes his neck to snuggle the side of his head to my cheek. *"No one's asked me tha in ages. I can't remember the last time. Thanks. Truly. Just being asked my opinion is a grand luxury."*

Warmth and affection fill the parts of my soul that I try to keep contained and off-limits to outsiders. When Connery sighs after inhaling the scent of my hair, the tense hold I've had on my body deflates. "You still haven't answered, though. Is there anything you need? I've never had a dog in the house before."

"This is more kindness than someone like me could ever expect," Connery tells me in his thick accent.

I get the feeling he's holding back. "You still didn't answer." When he shivers, I lean into his fur. "You're cold. Do dogs drink warm water? Would that be better?"

"Tea," Seven rules. "You need tea. Mommy makes the best tea."

Connery looks at her with such affection that I nearly tear up. She needs a dog so badly. This dog. Someone to love her, regardless. *"Truly? You're offering me tea?"* His big puppy eyes are filled with emotion, and when he speaks, his voice comes back choked. *"Tea would be grand. I'm cold to my bones."*

"A talking dog who drinks tea?" I kiss the top of his head. "Now I've seen everything."

Seven hops up, happy to be helpful. "I can make the tea!"

"Don't touch the stove!" I remind her. "You can get down the teabags, but I'll handle the kettle. You know the drill."

"Deal!" She scampers out of the bathroom.

Now that Seven can't witness my vulnerable moment, I run my fingers through the damp fur, my arms wrapping around Connery's neck just because I want to cuddle a dog. In my heart of hearts, I've always longed for extra snuggles from someone to whom I didn't have to justify my occasional weakness for affection. Part of my heart feels healed at the cuddle, settling an unrest that's been hard to quiet.

It would have been nice to have a dog growing up to get me through the rough times.

When I failed that social studies exam that, years later, I still don't forgive myself for.

When I couldn't sleep because Mom was working and I had to put Aashya to bed and explain to her what the term "towelhead" meant. And that no, she couldn't and shouldn't ask Mom to stop wearing her hijab.

When I finally got up the nerve to ask Jenny Gleeson to the school dance, and she looked at me with horror, then called me a dyke. It didn't matter that I'm actually bisexual. It only mattered that I was different, and apparently, that was scary to the girls in my school.

I really could have used a dog to snuggle back then.

And if I'm being honest, I could use those snuggles now, when the uncertainties of motherhood grip me around the throat and remind me that I have no idea what I'm doing.

"I hope you realize how spoiled you are," I scold

Connery good naturedly, kissing his face. "I haven't even made myself tea, yet here I am, about to fix a cup for a dog."

I can hear the male chuckle vibrating into my chest.

"Stay here," I tell him as I stand. "I'll make you a little bed out there and carry you to it. You shouldn't be putting pressure on that leg."

"Aye." Connery makes a point of sitting like a good boy, so I bend over and kiss the top of his head before I help Seven with the kettle.

The spare flowery comforter folded on the floor of the living room makes a fine bed for a dog, but carrying him there is a feat of brute strength for which I am ill-equipped.

I am halfway to the makeshift dog bed when the front door opens, and Jonathan sings my name through the house. "Zara, I..." But the sight of me carrying the giant dog stops him short. "Holy! Since when did you get a wolf? Or is he a bear?"

I nearly drop Connery onto the puddled comforter but thankfully manage a semi-gentle landing. "What? No, this is a dog."

Though, I'm not all that familiar with breeds and whatnot.

Jonathan's blond hair is swooshed in front, his fingers messing the styled dresses as he gapes at me. "No, Z. That is no dog. Out," he demands in a firm voice directed at Connery. "Sev, out you go, honey. Hurry!"

Connery sits up, fixing Jonathan with a look that tells him he's not going anywhere, and neither are we.

WE GOT A DOG

Seven does her usual run and jump into Jonathan's arms, but his expression doesn't hold its usual joy. "Papa Jonathan, we got a dog!"

"That's not a dog," Jonathan insists, angling her away from Connery. "It's a wolf or a bear, and it belongs outside." He shoots me a scolding look, because I am supposed to be the responsible one of the two of us.

I hold up my hands as I stand beside Connery. "I know he can't stay here forever. He was injured, Jonathan, so we..." But as I set out to explain my choices, my voice trails off sheepishly.

Did I seriously carry a wolf or a bear into my home? Are there really wild forest animals around here just roaming around?

Seven squirms her way down and skips to Connery, throwing her arms around his neck while he stares down

Jonathan in a way that isn't exactly threatening, but it's not inviting, either.

Jonathan's voice turns shrill. "Seven, get over here! Don't go near it like that." My bestie practically lives at the gym, and it shows when he's having an overprotective moment, like now.

Seven squints up at Jonathan as if he's being silly. "Oh, Papa Jonathan. This is Connery, my new dog. Isn't he perfect? We found him injured in a dark, spooky alley. He had no one, and he was crying, all alone. My poor baby-baby." She blinks up at her father figure with beautiful brown eyes the size of saucers.

Gotta love her theatrics.

She hugs Connery around the neck. "So we brought him home to live with us."

"To stay until Animal Control takes him," I remind her.

But it's like I didn't even speak. "We fed him, bathed him and wrapped his boo-boo." She shows Jonathan the bandage. "Poor baby, right?"

Jonathan runs his hand over his face. "I don't know what to say to this. It's a wolf, Seven. You realize that, right? And Connery? Where'd you come up with that name?"

It doesn't sound crazy at all when Seven shrugs and answers a simple, "He told me that's his name."

Jonathan squats to get on Seven's level, still standing on the welcome mat. "How about you go to your room and gather all the princess crowns you can find. I came over to play dress-up with my favorite girls, but I'm missing the most important elements. Can you find me a shawl, too? I'm thinking I should be the queen's grandmother this time."

Seven claps and squeals, kissing Jonathan's cheek as she races to her bedroom.

Connery makes to follow, but stops when Jonathan corrects him with a sharp, "Stay."

Connery's head turns to Jonathan with a cold stare. I can tell he doesn't like obeying Jonathan, so I explain things better. Connery doesn't like being told what to do, as if he's a dog. "Don't talk to him like that," I scold my best friend. Then to Connery, I explain, "Jonathan's nervous because you're in the house. He loves Seven, so if you could stay where he can see you until he gets used to you being around her, that would be super helpful for all involved."

Connery meets my brown eyes with his blue ones, and I can tell he's wondering if Jonathan is safe to have in the house.

I nod, my hand running over Connery's fur when he comes to my side. "Jonathan is a very safe person. Nothing to worry about." I glance up at my best friend. "Both of you."

Jonathan regards the two of us warily, his panic coming out in a sharp whisper. "What is going on with you? Miss looks twelve times before you cross the street, wash your hands before supper and vacuum every single day is letting a wolf off the streets into your home and around Sev?" He jabs his pointer finger at Connery in accusation. "That's a wolf, Zara! It's the biggest wolf I've ever seen in my life."

My hands move to my hips, though why I'm being defiant, I can't say. Being challenged pushes me to double down on this bad decision. "Connery is fine, J. And he's not staying. I was just going to call Animal Control."

Jonathan motions to my cell phone on the coffee table. "Well, what are you waiting for?"

I repeat his words in a mocking tone because that's my best quip at the moment. But when I locate the number and connect the call, all I get is their afterhours answering machine.

My neck shrinks as I pocket my phone. "Um, whoops. I didn't realize they closed at a certain time. Probably should have called them before bathing the dog and feeding him."

"Do you even have dog food here?"

I grimace. "Connery likes my murgh makhani."

Jonathan fixes me with a curious stare before devolving into giggles.

I am just stressed enough to lend my hysteria to the mix, a bubbly sound escaping my lips to match his.

"You have a wolf in your house, Z," he points out between breaths.

Oh my word, I have a wolf in the house. My laughter

sounds unbalanced when the tension breaks. "I carried him inside! And he's probably going to have to stay the night!"

Jonathan shimmies his shoulders. "Slumber party!"

I shake my head. "You don't have to stay the night."

Jonathan bumps his fist to mine, knowing that I prefer fist-bumps to hugs. "I'm not leaving my two favorite girls alone in the house with a wolf." He chuckles all over again. "A wolf! That'll never stop being funny, now that it's less terrifying. A wolf who prefers Indian food."

"I should probably get some dog food." I feel winded, now that I've explained things to Jonathan. My best friend is a good five inches taller than me, and his skin is several shades lighter. He smells of too much cologne, but it's never unpleasant. "How was your date last night?" I ask him. "I haven't had a chance to check my messages."

Jonathan moves us to the couch, where we plop ungracefully on the red cushions. He tugs a pillow onto his lap, so he has something to hold while we chat. "Don't go talking all normal when you let a wolf in the house."

Connery limps to my side and sits on my feet, warming them without being asked. His maw rests on my thigh in a manner that's protective, but not aggressively so. My fingers fall to Connery's massive head, stroking his fur without telling my hand to do so. "Spill it, Jonathan. Tell me the important stuff: how hot, how interesting, how emotionally unavailable."

Jonathan smirks, sitting sideways on the couch to face

me. "Well, he was a tall drink of water, but zero sense of humor. I did my first date story—you know, the one where I dropped my lemonade on the boat—and he didn't even smile."

I guffaw because no matter the issue, I am always on Jonathan's side. "That is one of your best hilarious stories."

"No sense of humor but handsome and employed, so it wasn't a total bust. No date number two in our future, though."

"Well, you're also handsome and employed *with* a sense of humor, so I don't see what the guy from last night might bring to the table."

He studies his immaculately kept cuticles. "The curse of being eternally perfect is that it's just not worth settling down."

I clink an imaginary glass of wine to his, and then we drink our air together, toasting our perpetual singlehood that neither of us is all that concerned about changing.

When the kettle sings, Connery follows me to the kitchen while Jonathan keeps a close eye on the two of us. He swings himself up to sit on my counter, as per usual when I'm fixing tea for the evening.

I make three cups and then discretely put a tea bag into a shallow bowl for Connery. I pour the water and then add fresh mint leaves and honey while Jonathan finishes up his account of the boring date from last night.

When he finishes, he sighs. "So, no Addison, eh?"

My expression closes off. "No Addison. Her mother

informed me they had 'a thing.' No specifics, just that the playdate is cancelled with no hope of rescheduling. But Addison told Seven that it's because Sev is trans."

Jonathan's upper lip curls. "Snot-nosed bigots. How's my little cupcake holding up?"

I shrug. "Well, we accidentally adopted a dog on the way home, so that's been a nice distraction."

Jonathan chuckles. "Ah. I see why you turned into a pushover since the last time I saw you. Though, I've got to admit, that's the tamest wolf I've ever seen."

"How many wolves have you seen in your long, wild career in advertising?"

"One," Jonathan admits, smirking at Connery. The two are starting to relax around each other, now that Jonathan is certain that Connery won't maul us, and Connery is certain that Jonathan won't take us away from him.

I blow on the shallow bowl of tea and then set it on the floor while Seven scampers back down the steps. "It's still hot, sweetheart. Wait a few minutes for it to cool, or you'll burn your tongue."

Jonathan sits up straighter on my countertop. "Um, what are you doing? Did you just... Are you serving the wolf a bowl of tea?"

My lips purse while I try to defend my actions, but I think I'm beyond logic at this point. "Connery prefers tea."

Jonathan barks out a laugh. "Really?"

Seven trots into the kitchen with an armload of tiaras,

shawls, jewelry, and ribbons. "Connery, I brought you a crown! It's pink and it lights up. Hold still."

Connery regards the crown warily, but as it is Seven's wish, he complies, wearing the crown even though I can tell by his fidgety nature that he hates it.

The four of us dress up in our royal best, and then sit down for tea at the table, munching on the scones I baked yesterday so Addison and Seven could have high tea, like fancy ladies.

"Orange chocolate chip," Jonathan comments after a bite. "Delicious. Queen Zara, you're the best chef in the land."

I love the look of Jonathan trussed up in clip-on earrings, a crown, a pink shawl and three gawdy pearl necklaces. His date last night let someone truly special slip through his fingers.

Connery sits between Seven and me, lapping at his tea and coiling his furry tail around my leg. It is hands down the best teatime of my life, sharing it with my new dog.

We do all the things Seven had planned for her play-date with Addison after we eat dinner, including making it through the longest game of Monopoly that ever was.

Connery fell asleep with his head on my thigh after Jonathan bought his first hotel. He continued snuggling me until I thankfully went bankrupt two hours later.

By the time the sun set, Seven was fighting sleep, determined to win the game while Jonathan held on strong to his last three properties he hadn't mortgaged.

"I think it's bedtime, little cupcake," he tells Seven after her second yawn.

After a fair attempt at cajoling her way out of bedtime, Jonathan promises to read her two stories with plenty of different voices thrown in if she can brush her teeth, get her pajamas on, and brush her hair in the next five minutes.

It's the quickest Seven has moved in days. She dashes up the steps while I try to convince myself that I should clean up the board game before doing the last thing on my to-do list for the night.

"To bed with you, Queen Zara," Jonathan insists in a regal voice. Then he stands and kisses my forehead. "I'll put Seven to bed and I'll put away the game. You go to sleep."

"But I..."

"I'm staying over tonight. It'll be far more fun seeing you get eaten by a wolf in person rather than reading about it in the news."

I nod, grateful for whenever he stays over. I don't mind being the only adult in the house, but every now and then, it's a relief to know that if something goes wrong, it's not all on me to figure out the answer.

"I need to go out for a quick errand first," I tell him, shooting him a knowing look.

Jonathan's hackles raise. "Zara, don't. Let it go. Addison's mom isn't the first bigot, and she won't be the last.

Whatever you're thinking of won't solve anything. It never does."

He knows me too well, just as he understands that when I rummage in the kitchen for what I need, grab my keys and my black hoodie instead of my red winter jacket, there is no talking me out of serving up justice in my own circuitous way. "Julie left my kid in tears. I'm not about to look the other way on that."

Jonathan reaches for the impassioned logic he's repeated often, albeit fruitlessly. "You're demanding perfection of the world, Zara, instead of progress. Progress takes time. Decades. Sometimes a century. And progress is happening. It's coming slower than any of us would like, but twenty years ago, no way would you have been able to petition the school board for any of the things Seven needs."

"Yeah, and I was denied most of them. That's not progress."

Jonathan is more level-headed than I am, especially when I am angry and on a mission. "All I'm saying is that Julie is doing the best she can with the limited information she has."

I roll my eyes. "She has access to the internet, Jonathan. She has a world's worth of information at her fingertips. She's burying her head in the sand and selectively educating herself. That's not 'doing her best.' I get that your Zen acceptance of people needing time to come around helps you, and I'm not going to argue how very wrong I believe you are. Julie's not interested in educating herself or her daughter. She wants her world small, with only people who look and behave like her."

Jonathan regards me with pity, as if my anger is something that holds me back instead of propelling me forward. It's then that he reaches for the wisdom he often bestows upon me when I least want to hear it. "You can't solve it all in a night, Zara."

I've long since stopped arguing with him when he tries to infuse me with his eerie calm. But in my heart, I grumble at the limitations I refuse to put on myself. "I'm going."

Jonathan holds up his hands in surrender, conceding the fight. "You do you, boo. But I maintain that progress takes time, and it's not helped by doing your Instant Karma thing."

"Maybe not, but it helps me vent the steam out of my boiling anger so I don't lose it on someone who doesn't deserve it like Julie does."

He motions between the two of us. "You know the deal. If you go out as Instant Karma to handle business your way, then in the morning, we handle things my way."

I let loose a dramatic sigh. "Yeah, yeah. I'll do my time writing yet another useless letter to the governor, to a state senator, and then to congress. I know, I know." I hate that Jonathan makes me write letters, as if those in power actually read them. Even when they do give them a glance, we are written off and sent a form letter, thanking us for reaching out.

Nothing changes. Nothing gets better for my daughter.

But that's the agreement Jonathan and I made. If I go out as Instant Karma to wreck the night of the person who made my baby cry, then I have to do the slow-moving work of writing in letters to people he believes can affect actual change in policies for us.

I'll believe it when I see it.

"Be back in twenty," I promise grabbing the hoodie I keep in the closet for just such occasions. I move to the kitchen and rummage in the pantry for the supplies. Then I kneel and kiss Connery, who whines at my impending absence. "Keep an eye on Seven?"

Connery nods, kissing my knuckles.

Jonathan sighs. "Go on. Get it out of your system. You know I'm good for bail money."

4

INSTANT KARMA

started with the alter ego when I was in middle school and some jerks were picking on Aashya. It didn't dawn on me that popping all their bike tires was wrong. The administration of the school was doing nothing. I actually heard one of them say, "Kids will be kids."

No. She was the only brown kid in all the classes for her grade, and she was constantly picked on for it. That's not a "kids will be kids." That's a "kids need to be held accountable."

I learned that the adults weren't ready to do that, so I popped the bike tires of each one of my sister's bullies.

It was so satisfying, doing something evil in secret, paying evil for evil instead of hoping that one day they'd grow up. They made Aashya cry, so they got to be sad their bicycles didn't work.

Fair's fair.

My black hoodie is my uniform because the hood is oversized and hangs over my face enough to conceal my identity from afar. I zip it up and feel the satisfying shudder that always comes over me when I don my armor. I inhale new oxygen, letting it cleanse my irritation because tonight, my anger will do what it needs to do.

What no one else in my state's government is willing to do.

Tonight, my anger has a purpose.

My black hoodie is cotton and thin, but the cold doesn't touch me. Instant Karma doesn't care about things like snow. Instant Karma wants the people who judge and ostracize children to suffer. I am not Zara when I wear this hoodie.

I am Instant Karma.

I walk at an unremarkable pace down the street out of the middle-class area to the trappings of suburbia.

Do I know where Addison lives?

Yes, I do.

Do I know what sort of car Julie drives?

Yes, I do.

The BMW is silver and sleek, begging to be messed with as I walk through the wintry weather toward my mark.

Instant Karma is the supervillain name I worked out with Jonathan and Aashya many years ago. When someone thinks they're going to get away with being an ass, Instant Karma pounces. It's not deadly, and mostly it's to curb my own wrath at always getting handed the raw end of the deal in life.

Jonathan says I have anger issues.

I don't much care if I do. Pouring a baggie full of sugar in Julie's gas tank is the only way to vent the steam that is always building under the surface, pushing me further and further over the edge of reason. Mess with me, and I usually just grumble under my breath and walk away. Mess with my daughter?

Sugar in the gas tank, at minimum. Make my baby cry, and you get to cry the next day.

It's not hard to flood a person's backyard without them noticing. Crank the hose just enough that the home-owners can't hear the water flowing and position it out of sight of any windows. I smile as I picture Julie's perfect backyard a mess of puddles and ice in the morning.

Maybe their basement will leak. Then she'll cry.

She'd better feel overwhelmed and anxious. Scared, even. That's what she did to my daughter with her bigotry. Did she think I was going to look the other way? Slink off into the background where she believes we belong?

The permanent marker lives in the pocket of my hoodie and makes itself useful scripting in a large graffiti font "Bigot".

Do I have a compact emergency window puncher in the pocket of my hoodie? Why, Instant Karma never leaves home without one. I've done this enough times that I know how to shatter a car window without making too much noise in the process. Bringing the hose from the backyard to the side of the house that is shrouded from the neighbors is easy. Feeding the hose through the shattered window to flood the interior of the car is just plain fun.

I don't know how to be a mother, and I'm not sure this is the right way, but I do know I cannot turn a blind eye to my baby girl's tears. She was looking forward to this play-date and didn't deserve this sort of treatment. Kids have it hard enough without adults getting in the way and being jerks.

I want to inflict more damage after I return the hose to continue flooding the backyard, but I know I can't do much more without risking getting caught.

Eyeing the mailbox, I reason I should probably quit while I'm ahead, so I turn on my heel and walk slowly back to my condo, knowing that by morning Julie will feel the brunt of Instant Karma's wrath.

5

FIST-BUMPS

I shiver when I walk into the condo, fixing Jonathan with a weak smile. "Finished with my walk."

Jonathan's jaw ticks with unhappiness. "Glad to hear it. You know, Seven doesn't need you to avenge her. She needs you to hold her while she's hurting."

My brows push together as I hang up my hoodie in the closet. "I did exactly that when she got off the bus. I can do both, you know."

"You always do. Now sit and write. We'll do it together."

I hate this part, but I do it to pacify Jonathan, to make him feel like we're not always going to be dealt a losing hand by those in power. We write three letters each, detailing the various laws that keep our girl from being truly free, and our wishes that these laws be repealed.

When Jonathan finishes sealing the last envelope, he shoots me a look of barely contained intrigue. "Sugar in the gas tank?"

I shrug. "It's a classic for a reason. And flooded the backyard."

"Bash in any windows?"

"Just a car window."

"No house windows?"

I roll my eyes. "I only did that once, and I don't regret it. Anyone who calls you the f-word gets what they get, which is a broken front window." That bit of vandalism had been particularly satisfying.

Jonathan softens, taking in my controlled upset with grace. "I love you, you know."

"I know." It's one of the few constant facts that keeps me upright. Oxygen, gravity, and the fact that Jonathan and I will always have each other.

He fixes me with a cautious stare, speaking slowly. "And I don't need you to protect me."

"I know." That has never been true, but I let him think it is because that's what he needs to believe. He might be solid and sculpted now, but I knew Jonathan back when he was the ninety-pound freshman with braces and bad acne.

I stand to wipe down the counters, and Jonathan moves the teacups to the sink, washing them by hand.

When he finishes, he holds up his finger as if to scold me. "I'm going to hug you, and you're going to pretend you're the type of person who lets people hug her."

I give him the dead eye. "I'm fine, Jonathan. Julie's the one who's going to be crying in the morning."

Jonathan takes a step toward me, as if I am a wild animal in need of calming. "Your daughter was ostracized yet again because of bigotry. That stings deeper than people realize."

I cross my arms over my chest. "I'm no stranger to bigotry. I'm a brown-skinned bisexual woman, which is the only thing people see when they look at me."

Jonathan takes another step. "And that hurt turns to rage inside of you quicker than you take the time to deal with any of it."

I motion to the front door. "I dealt with it. Julie's going to have a bad day because she gave my little girl a bad day. Instant Karma."

Jonathan runs a hand through his hair. "But you're landing on anger, and you never move off that island. You felt the anger. You acted on the anger. Good. Fine. Now it's time to feel the other things."

I hate this conversation we have all too often. "Like what?"

"Like sadness. Like disappointment. Like frightened. Like all the other things that come from this sort of behavior when it's aimed at your child. It can't always be anger. It can't always be vengeance. We're all at the beginning of our kindness education on something, Zara. Julie's learning curve directly affects the girls I love. If it stings me, I know it stings you."

My hip juts to the side. "I'm sure I was a shade of all those things when the news first hit me. But anger means action, and that's what was needed."

Jonathan's arms hang at his sides. "And I'm not saying you're wrong."

I throw my hands up. "Then what are you saying?"

Jonathan lets out a heavy sigh, as if I'm the kid who will never understand fractions in class. "I'm saying what I always say to you. That you can't solve it all in a night. I guess I'm saying that your anger is your armor, but it only protects you so much. When that armor comes off and you want to talk about any of those other things that creep in when life is unfair like this, I'm here and I'll listen, just like you do for me." He fixes me with a soft smile. "You know, the listening you do right before you go off and key someone's car."

I smack my forehead. "Ugh. That's what I should've done to Julie. Next time."

Jonathan and I share a chuckle and a fist-bump instead of the hug I know he wants to give me. Like it'll fix everything. He thinks that with one squeeze, all the emotions I don't want to touch are going to come flooding out my tear ducts all because of a simple hug.

The thing is, there's a real danger of that happening, so we stick to limited hugs because I need to get out of bed in the morning. I need to have breakfast on the table. I don't have the space to fall apart and admit that there are horrible things in life that I will never be able to protect my child from experiencing.

I don't do well with helpless. I'm better with action.

And subject changes. "Where's Connery?"

Jonathan jerks his thumb toward Seven's bedroom. "She's reading him a bedtime story. *Matilda* again."

My hand goes over my heart. "That's just about the cutest thing. She hates reading out loud."

Jonathan beams at me. "I know. Connery is her new therapy dog. Kids who have trouble reading in public read to a dog and it helps them gain confidence. I was going to take Sev to the library to read to their therapy dog next weekend."

Okay, that deserves a hug. But still I hang back. "Thank you. I never thought of that."

Jonathan grins at me. "That's why there's two of us in this. It pays to be the drag queen for library story time. I have all the hookups."

What I would do without Jonathan, I will never know. He's been by my side ever since I cut the straps off the backpack of the kid who was bullying him back in middle school. He doesn't need me to stand up for him now that he's a full-grown man who's been through therapy and come out the other side with his head higher.

He needs me to hug him occasionally.

I'm working on it.

He drives an hour outside of the state once a month to

read to children, dressed in his full drag. In our state, drag is not allowed around children because apparently reading to children is scary and salacious if you're a man dressed as Dorothy from *The Wonderful Wizard of Oz*.

Assholes.

None of the protestors ever signed up to read to the children for story time. None of the policymakers do that regularly either. But now it's this precious thing they need to stir up a fight about, so Jonathan reads to children in another state, where he and his wigs are welcome.

They don't care about the kids; they care about a man wearing lipstick in public.

The scandal.

Jonathan chucks my shoulder, letting me off the hook, as usual. "I'll put Sev to bed. You take a minute and decompress."

My shoulders drop in gratitude. "Thanks." I kiss his cheek, because that's a gesture I was raised with and am thus a bit more comfortable doling out to my bestie.

Jonathan trots to Seven's room, giving me the space to wind down for the night. I move into my gray-walled bedroom (that I really should have painted something more interesting when we moved in here), and grab up my fuzzy pajama pants and a silk pink camisole. I take my time washing my face and brushing my teeth, tired from the long day when I emerge to find Connery waiting for me outside the door.

A childish thrill zips through me. I always wanted to

have a pet, but my mother forbade it. I understood (eventually). She was a busy single mom. But now that I happen to have a dog in the house, images of me as a little girl drawing pictures of the dog I wanted to keep for my very own flood my brain.

I should bring in the comforter from the living room that Connery was supposed to be using as a bed, but I find myself patting my mattress twice. "You want to sleep in my bed with me?"

"A *bed?*" he inquires wistfully, as if I've offered him a cloud to sleep upon. *"I was going to guard the door for ye."*

I frown at my door. "Um, you can do that if you want. Is that a dog thing?"

"It's a me thing. I don't know any other way."

Compassion wells in me when I think of the hard life he must've lived before he came into our home. "Well, this is a nice, safe neighborhood. Nothing scary is going to happen tonight that you need to guard us from." I pat the mattress with a smile. "You can rest, Connery. Give yourself the space to be injured."

"On a mattress?" He eyes the space longingly.

"Sure. Might be more comfortable than the hard floor."

Connery limps forward, but whines because he can't seem to get up with his injured leg.

With my last bit of energy, I heft up the heavy wolf-bear-dog and rest him on the side of my queen bed, going so far as to tuck him in under the covers.

I slide under the comforter on the other side and turn off the lamp, wasting no time cuddling up to the furry wonder to which I am rapidly growing attached. Connery sighs happily, letting me spoon his massive body as he rests his head on my pillow. My cheek presses to his fur, warming me far more than the thin walls and drafty windows ever could.

Emotion I didn't want to feel in front of Jonathan (or ever) begins to well up in me.

Jonathan was right about all the things he said were there that I covered over with anger.

I am disappointed in Julie. Seven is a child, and she's teaching her own girl that there are the "right" kind of people to hang out with and the "wrong" kind, based on arbitrary measurements that ought not be passed from generation to generation.

I am sad that my little girl's feelings were hurt, and there's no way to heal them. She knows that she is different, and that some people will always see that difference as bad, instead of fun, or a simple fact of life.

And beneath all of that, a shudder of fear rushes through me that I really didn't want to feel. I hug Connery tighter, burying my face in his clean fur to fend off all the times I was dealt a raw deal, and now I get to watch my daughter go through the same thing.

I'm afraid of so many things I cannot control.

I'm afraid I'll let my sister down, raising her child in ways she might have done differently.

I'm afraid my mom would be disappointed in my job choice because she wanted me to be a surgeon, but that was never me. I was supposed to be the smart one, the one to go to an important school and bring us all up to a more respectable socioeconomic level.

I'm afraid that one day, the snubs and hurtful words directed at my little girl will become actual sticks and actual stones lobbed at her with no hint of mercy.

I'm afraid that this fear will force us to play small, to shrink our dreams so we don't stand out.

I'm afraid of so many things.

Connery rolls ungracefully to face me. *"You're upset."*

I'm glad it's dark, with only the moonlight filtering in through the gaps in the curtains to highlight the nuances of our faces. "I'm f-failing," I admit to him in a whisper, hoping the night will swallow my admission so my biggest fear doesn't come true in the daylight. "My baby is... Seven is... And I can't do anything to make it better." I don't have the right words, but my dog doesn't pull away simply because I'm not good at this.

Connery studies my vulnerability that only happens in the dark, and apparently only with a dog. He licks the tip of my nose and then smooths his maw across my cheek, not saying anything to try to cheer me up or brush aside my rampant insecurities. He lets me hold onto him, my brand-new beacon of safety that I never saw coming.

I don't know why it's possible for me to open up to him and not anyone else. I guess that's the magic of animals.

I don't dip further into the grief, having hit the furthest edges of my limit already. Instead, I hold onto my dog, hoping that in the morning, life doesn't feel quite so heavy.

Connery's good paw drapes over my waist under the covers. I can tell he's beyond the point of exhaustion when he mutters a quiet, *"Mattress. Bed. Thanks."*

I close my eyes as I mutter a grateful, "If you don't eat me in my sleep. I'll let you stay here forever."

"Deal." Connery chuckles, reminding me that something about this dog is very, very strange indeed.

6

VISITOR

I toss and turn with the best of them, rarely sleeping in one position for very long. I keep a notepad on my nightstand so I can scribble down anything I've forgotten to take care of, which is always something. My sheets are always a wadded, tangled mass by the morning.

Except for today.

My alarm wakes me at its usual 5:30am, but instead of popping out of bed, I turn off the annoying sound and roll over, returning to Sleepy Town. I'm one of those women who are perpetually chilly, but when I snuggle up to Connery, the heat he sends me is a balm to my soul.

I wrap my arms around his body and throw a leg over his haunches, cuddling as close as possible so I can absorb the warmth he radiates. I can't help the contented noise that sighs out of me, nor can I keep myself awake as I drift back to sleep, snuggled up to my furry body pillow.

He's just so precious. If this is what I've been missing, not having a dog in the house, then I have been seriously deprived.

I was going to wake up early so I could make Addison and Seven pancakes and bacon, but I think we're all going to enjoy our Saturday morning lie in.

It feels like a breath and a blink that the sun rouses me to wake, but in reality, it's a full two hours later.

Two hours of deep sleep.

Two hours of holding this dog and letting his steady breaths match my heartbeat.

Two hours of bliss.

I cringe as I finally sit up and stretch out my torso. I know I have to call Animal Control. This dog isn't mine. Plus, if Jonathan is correct and this is actually a wolf, then I really shouldn't get attached.

Except it's already too late. When I sit up, Connery moves his head to my side, his tail wagging as if waiting for my cue to start the day. I wonder how long he's been awake, just lying there patiently. I cradle his head in my hands and bring his face up to kiss his forehead. "Morning, snuggle bunny."

Connery licks my cheek. *Tha was the best night of sleep of my life.*

I grin at him. "Me, too."

My shower is quick before I pull on a pair of jeans and

my standard black t-shirt. As I brush my hair, I can hear Seven's tiny feet pattering across the floor in the kitchen while Jonathan sings horrifically off-key.

Man, I really did sleep in. That's a first.

Connery sticks tight to my side after I lower him from the bed to the floor. He can't put pressure on his front paw, poor thing, so he limps by my side as we move out into the kitchen.

The sizzle of bacon is the best alarm clock, waking me more fully as the scent hits my nose. "What do we have here?" I ask the two. Jonathan is wearing my pink apron with brown polka dots, and Seven is clad in her pink princess gown pajamas with a play chef's hat flopping on her head. "Turkey bacon with magical chocolate chip pancakes," Jonathan informs me. The sofa pulls out into a bed that he often crashes on when he stays the night, and I can see by a peek into the living room, noting the folded blankets on the nicely reassembled couch, that that's exactly what he did, so we wouldn't be alone this morning.

I never forget how lucky I am to have him as my best friend.

I clasp my hands under my chin. "Oo! What makes the pancakes magical?"

Seven does a twirl while she answers. "The chocolate chips grant wishes."

I wait until she finishes her twirl and then I scoop her up, peppering her face with kisses. "It worked! You're my wish, and here you are."

Seven giggles while I shower her with kisses.

The moment I set her down, Seven wraps her arms around Connery's thick neck.

My gosh, they are precious. Connery leans into her affection, his eyes closing in reverence because he clearly understands just how wonderful this little girl is.

Jonathan flips the pancakes and then pours me a cup of tea with a spoonful of honey—just the way I like it. "For you, not your dog," he clarifies with a silly grin.

The moment Seven releases her grip on Connery, I let him out into the backyard, grateful he didn't pee in the house. I have no idea how to train a dog, so I'm glad this one seems to know the basics already.

Jonathan kisses the tip of my nose just to be sweet. Every now and then he does domestic things for me, and we both get a kick out of it. "Morning, Sunshine. I can't believe you slept in. I checked in on you this morning to make sure the wolf didn't eat you, and you were sound asleep."

I inhale the fragrant tea, grateful to start the weekend like this. "I haven't slept that hard in ages."

"Still taking Connery to Animal Control?"

I pause as the mug warms my hands. "I mean, if they're not open after five on a weekday, I highly doubt they keep weekend hours. I'll call on Monday."

Jonathan shoots me a knowing grin. "Uh-huh."

Seven scampers to the table with a plate of two pancakes and two pieces of bacon. She likes things to match. If there was fruit, she would select two strawberries to go with the two pancakes—no more, no less.

Jonathan plates me a small stack and some bacon, looking on his handiwork with pride. "Look at these pancakes. So fluffy."

I lean up on my toes to kiss the tip of his nose. "You're going to make some guy very lucky someday. Thanks for making breakfast."

"Thanks for sleeping in. Makes me worry less about you."

I frown as I sit at the table with my breakfast. Jonathan shouldn't worry about me. I'm on top of things. The bills are paid, Seven is getting good grades and has a solid attendance record. She's not behind on doctor visits or the dentist.

"There's nothing for you to worry about, J. I've got this."

Jonathan sits beside me after turning off the burner and plating himself a huge stack of pancakes with bacon on the side. "I have no doubt."

But his words linger even as the interruption of the doorbell rings through the house.

Jonathan shakes his head when I rise. "I've got it. You eat."

"What did I do to deserve you?"

Jonathan winks at Seven. "I think it was all those years you helped me study for exams, woke me up for work when I had two jobs, and in general were literally awesome."

"Literally," Seven agrees. "Papa Jonathan is so grateful; he's going to bake a chocolate cake with me today."

Jonathan squints at Seven before mussing her hair. "Don't push it."

He moseys to the front door in his khakis and dress shirt—ever photo ready, as is his way. "Can I help you?"

"Milk maid," announces a man's voice, bending my ears enough that I stand.

"Stay put," I tell Seven as I move to the front door.

The man is clad in fitted black trousers, a pinstriped white dress shirt tailored to his lean yet muscular physique, paired with suspenders. His black hair is styled to stand up to the left, looking a mixture of windblown and perfectly in place. His angular features would be handsome if his demeanor wasn't so haughty.

His lavender eyes land on me. "Is he here?"

My arms cross over my chest while my feet move shoulder width apart. I tilt my head to Jonathan. "This is the only 'he' here. You've got the wrong address."

The man inhales deeply as if smelling an invisible rose. "No, he's here alright. Don't worry; he's safe with me. I won't bring him in."

Seven's tiny voice stiffens my spine. "Oo! I love your suspenders. So gentlemanly."

"You've got the wrong address." I hold the edge of the door, effectively dismissing the man as I slam it in his face.

7

THE GENTLEMAN

Jonathan and I exchange a "what the heck was that about" look. Jonathan trots to the backdoor and lets Connery back inside. "When in doubt, turn on the security system."

It's a joke, clearly, because I don't have a security system (thought I mentally put that on my list). He runs his hand over Connery's fur. "Stranger at the door, Connery. If he comes back, you can feel free to bite his leg off."

Connery gives Jonathan an answering bark and then licks Seven's cheek, which is sticky with syrup. He's kissing her, sure, but he's also cleaning her up like a cutesy dog nanny you might see in a cartoon.

I love it.

No, I can't call Animal Control today. They're probably not even open on the weekends. And if they were…

Monday. I'll wait until Monday.

A Monday in the distant future.

Though, as I feed Connery a piece of bacon from my plate, I recognize the lie even as I tell it to myself.

A slow knock starts at the front door. Over and over, the ominous rhythm drums through the house.

Seven jumps up from her seat. "I'll get it!"

Jonathan and I stand as one, and together we tell her, "No, I'll get it."

Seven giggles whenever we do that. Hazards of being best friends for this many years, I guess. Sometimes we finish each other's sentences, and other times, we share a brain and fight over who gets to use it.

I throw up my trump card. "My house. I'll get it."

But Jonathan goes with me to the front door while Connery sniffs the entrance to, I dunno, check for bombs or something. Connery is quite intent on locating the source of this smell.

I peer through the peephole and see the dapper guy standing on the stoop. I frown that he is still trying to interrupt our lovely breakfast.

"Is there a problem?" I call through the closed door.

The man on the other side fixes the peephole with a wicked grin that shows off his pearly white teeth. "There won't be a problem at all if you hand him over. Trust me, you don't want him in your home when the authorities catch wind you're housing him. I'm here to do you a favor."

Seven squeals. "Oo! It's the gentleman!"

Jonathan turns his head to Seven. "No. It's a wolf in sheep's clothing." Then he shoots an apologetic look to Connery. "No shade to our present company." Jonathan moves to the table to make sure Seven stays put. "Gentleman don't keep on knocking on a lady's door once they've been turned away. That's called being creepy."

"I heard that!" the man sings from the other side of the door.

Connery's ears perk up, an excited whine coming out of him in spurts. I can tell he's excited to see whoever is out there.

I press my palm to the door. "He. You said 'he'. Are you talking about Connery? Because he's not going with you, either."

There's a pause, and then the man's voice answers without a hint of the playfulness he was displaying as if it was a stylish outfit. "You must let me in. If you've got Connery inside, you're in grave danger. You're a mother, yes?"

"Yes." I legally adopted Seven upon my sister's request, taking our sweet girl in after Aashya's death.

I turn my chin over my shoulder and see that Seven is beaming at me.

While crossing her eyes.

The goof.

She's my sister's kid, is who she is. The silliness seals it.

The man's voice lowers while Connery paws at the door. "You don't want this blowing up in your home in front of your child. They don't care who they hurt. They want Connery. Housing him is a crime." Before my blood pressure spikes, the man offers a clear, "But I can help you."

My lips purse while I consider letting this man into my home for reasons that sound completely unreasonable. No one is going to arrest me for helping a stray. That's ridiculous.

But even the hint of danger coming near Seven is a chance I cannot take.

Before I can answer, the doorknob turns, even though I know it's locked.

I gasp, but before I can counter the action, the door swings open as if the man in suspenders owns my spare key.

Only he doesn't appear to have it. My door just opened for him.

He shoots me an apologetic look. "It's poor manners to burst into someone's house without invitation," he says over my shoulder to Seven. "Your father is right. But this supersedes the rules."

Seven squeals happily. "I knew he was a gentleman!"

Jonathan scoops Seven in his arms, thank goodness. "Connery, get him!"

But Connery doesn't appear to know that particular command. He sniffs the man's shoes and barks a few times before the man nods with compassion in his eyes. "I know you're hiding in Common. That's why they sent me. I'm supposed to bring you in." He lifts his pant leg to show a bit of rope tied around his ankle. "They've got me on a tether, so they can lock me back up once I find you and bring you in."

It looks like an ordinary piece of rope to me.

I frown at my dog. "Connery, you know this guy?"

Connery swings his head to me and limps to my side, running his body along the outside of my leg. I can tell he doesn't want to speak aloud. He hasn't done that in front of Jonathan yet, so I know that shock is still coming.

"He's hurt," the man says, stating the obvious.

"No kidding," I retort. "We found him yesterday all bloody, so we brought him here to give him a little break from whatever was stupid enough to pick a fight with him."

The man sticks out his hand. "Thank you. Truly. Most would have left him for dead." He gives me a small bow when I don't shake his hand. "I'm Bodhi, at your service." He steps in and shuts the door behind him with a wary look. "For the moment, at least."

My fists clench and my gait widens because a stranger just entered my home without permission. "Jonathan, take Sev out the back."

But before he can do that, Bodhi raises his hand. "I wouldn't do that. Our best bet is to lockdown. If the house is being watched, then they'll know if one of you leaves."

My voice climbs to a shriek. "Why would anyone be watching the house?"

Bodhi motions to his ankle again. "Because I have a tether. I thought I explained that already." He sighs and then addresses Connery. "I'm sorry, old friend. They only let me out if I promised to lead them to you. But obviously I have no intention of turning you over to them. I only took the job because I knew that if I didn't, they would send an inmate who would actually do as he was told. We can't have that. I just wasn't counting on you being injured." He frowns at Connery's bandage. "No matter. I'll defend the house myself. Then we can be on our way."

Connery barks twice, but unlike the other times, I don't understand what he's saying.

Bodhi shakes his head. "I cannot protect them long-term. You know a child is a liability."

Seven barks at him as if she is a dog. Then she says in a superior tone, "Don't talk about me as if I don't know what 'liability' means."

That's right. My baby's smart.

Jonathan's voice deepens, doing the man thing where he gets all authoritative and people actually listen. As if he's not a giant pushover who likes to wear my pink fuzzy slippers on movie nights. "Walk us through it all right now or get out. If someone is coming, we need to know."

Except I very much want to know nothing about any of it if it means Connery might have to leave us.

8

ORPHANS

Bodhi's leonine body is graceful as he moves into the kitchen, sitting in my spot at the table and helping himself to a piece of my bacon.

"Hey! That's mine."

Bodhi grimaces. "Apologies. It's been so long since I've had anything that didn't come in mush form. I quite forgot my manners."

Jonathan lifts his chin, indignant. "Don't eat off Zara's plate. I'll get you your own."

Apparently, Bodhi's staying for breakfast.

Connery barks at Bodhi until the newcomer holds his hands up after taking a bite off the plate Jonathan fixes for him. "Okay, fine. You want an explanation?" He motions to my dog. "Connery and I come from... somewhere else."

"Canada?" Seven guesses.

Bodhi smiles at Seven. "Somewhere even more magical, if you can believe it. A place called Crimshade." Then his expression turns grave. "But our world isn't without its problems. There's a disease filtering through the land. Whoever is infected is deemed disloyal to the throne. It's supposed to be nature's way of keeping the streets clean, if you know what I mean. If a person comes down with the traitor's disease, it's assumed they are plotting against the throne, so they are tossed in jail, where the disease ravages their body, and they slowly die."

I gape at Bodhi. "Are you insane? Don't talk about whatever nonsense that is in front of Seven. She's a child!" I turn to my baby. "Honey, that's not true. The world doesn't work like that."

Bodhi tilts his head at me. "It doesn't? Your world has never had a disease that disproportionately took down one sort of people? And that didn't please the more 'normal' populace? Is it really so strange to think that bigotry and inhumanity happen habitually among people who can't be bothered to care?" Bodhi fixes me with a knowing look. "That's right, pretty poppet. I used to surface in Common from time to time when my world proved too frustrating to bear. I know just how cruel your world can get, so don't stand there, feigning flabbergast that horrible things happen elsewhere too."

I open my mouth and then shut it.

Jonathan grips Seven tighter, and I know he's thinking about the same thing I am: the AIDS epidemic.

The two of us swallow hard. Jonathan has been HIV

positive for about a decade (though undetectable, thank goodness), and has seen widespread ostracization when people don't bother educating themselves. They assume he's contagious. They assume he's dying.

Some assume he deserves to live with it and die by it, because who he is might be wicked.

Rage rises in my sternum like acid reflux ready to turn into pure fire. But I've learned that my rage does Jonathan no good when it comes to this particular topic.

I clear my throat and struggle to keep my voice level. "So, what? Is Connery diseased with this traitor's sickness? Are you? Is that why you're wearing that piece of rope on your ankle?"

Connery flattens his belly to the floor and hides his head under the couch, whining pitifully.

Emotion chokes me as I flit to his side, lowering myself onto my knees so I can wrap my arms around him. "Hey, it's okay. Talk to me. I know you can." When he doesn't speak, guilt floods me. "I shouldn't have said it harsh like that. Traitor's sickness sounds like you did something to deserve it, when that's not how diseases work. I know you're good. I see you." I kiss his furry spine then rest my cheek atop his back. "Oh, honey."

Connery keeps his head under the couch. *"It's true,"* he tells me in his deep, beautiful voice.

I lift my head and lock eyes with Jonathan, who startles, jostling Seven in his arms. "See?" she giggles. "I told you Connery can talk. You didn't believe me."

"Did that dog just speak actual words?" Jonathan asks, paling at the question no one ever expects they will have to ask.

I gnaw on my lower lip before nodding at my best friend. "I didn't know how to tell you. Connery isn't a normal dog. That's why we can't take him to the shelter."

Sure. That's why. It's certainly not because I'm a softy at heart who turns into a puddle of goo around a cute dog.

Jonathan swallows hard, clinging to Seven, who is giddy at all the excitement. "Okay, then. Go on, Connery. We're listening. To a talking dog." I can tell Jonathan is on the verge of true panic.

My dog still has his head buried under the couch. *"My will was taken away when I became a man."*

Bodhi nods once, his angular jaw taut. "Shifters can be controlled if a mage casts a very horrible and powerful spell that takes away their will. The moment Connery was old enough to be useful to the throne, that's what they did to him."

I gasp at the horror, unable to land for too long on the fact that this isn't a dog; it's actually a man. Or both. I'm not completely sure just yet.

Connery continues. *"I was a slave to the throne, unable to shift or say no to the mage's commands. But then I came down with the disease. I knew I wasn't disloyal; t'wasn't possible. I didn't have the ability to do anything other than what the king's mage commanded. Me coming down with the traitor's disease would dismantle the whole belief system."* He shoves his head further under the couch. *"Pavma helped me escape."*

"Really?" Bodhi remarks. "I suspected he might be on our side, but I couldn't tell for certain."

Connery explains to us, *"Pavma is one of my soldiers. He took the emerald tha held my will and smashed it, gifting me back to myself so I couldn't terrorize the land anymore on the king's orders."*

Bodhi takes a step toward us but comes no closer when he sees my glare of distrust aimed at the stranger. He holds up his hands and directs his question toward my dog. "But why are you still an animal, Connery? I thought I would come to you and see you as yourself—the guy I grew up with in the orphanage. Are you still trapped?"

Connery whimpers pathetically, tugging on my heartstrings and forcing a whimper from Seven. *"The mage managed to collect the smashed bits of the emerald. I didn't realize he would still be able to control whether or not I could shift if the emerald was broken. I wanted out, so I ran, and now I'm forever this."*

"You couldn't have known," Bodhi says kindly, his eyes closing.

"Instead of letting them kill me, I escaped. I ran to Common." His tail tucks tight to his side. *"I want to die in peace, even if it's the traitor's disease tha takes me. I deserve all tha and more for what I did to the people under the royal influence."*

I throw my torso over Connery, hugging my wolf. Even

though I don't fully understand and am not sure I believe this entire thing, I know heartbreak and self-loathing when I see it. "You don't deserve this," I tell him, fully confident that, even though I don't know the whole story, I can cling to that much, at least. "You were being controlled."

Connery is firm that I am wrong. *"The prisons are filled with innocent, sick people because I put them there."*

"But you didn't have control over your mind or your body! How could that be your fault?"

Bodhi touches his finger to his chin as he observes us from above. "I'd listen to the lady, Connery. You never did listen to me." He glances around, his expression devoid of the laidback charm he oozed upon his arrival. "We need to leave this place. The soldiers who are searching for Connery won't care that you all didn't know about our world. They only care about containing the outbreak. Controlling the narrative of the outbreak. Connery is the key to it all. He couldn't have been disloyal to the throne, yet he has the traitor's disease." Bodhi's eyes fix on me. "And they very much care if anyone is caught aiding and abetting a fugitive. I settle for nothing less than absolute fireworks. If they come for us, defending your home won't be a gentle affair."

I snarl at Bodhi. "If what you're saying is true, then your world is sick. Hunting down a poor dog, thinking he might be disloyal to the throne? Crimshade is terrible."

Bodhi fixes me with a long stare, giving my denial time

to settle and quiet so my mind can make the leap past logic and into the realm of, dare I say it, magic.

Jonathan is always braver than I am and voices the conclusion before I can put words to my wondering. "Connery isn't a dog. He isn't a wolf. Not really." He clutches Seven tighter. He stares with concern down at our new furry addition. "What are you?"

Connery whines as he slides his head out from under the couch. He stares at me with beautiful blue eyes the color of a clear summer's sky, and darn if I don't care that he's not a normal dog. He's mine. He's the friend I've always wanted.

And in that moment, I can see it all. Connery belongs with us. We will love him and make sure he's looked after. I don't care if he's a magical creature. His home is right here in my arms.

I don't expect someone as haughty as Bodhi to be gentle with my shock, but his reply comes out measured and careful. "You have shapeshifters in your world, yes?"

My nose crinkles. "In books, sure, but not for real."

Bodhi tilts his head at me. "Connery is a shapeshifter. His other form is a forty-year-old orphan-turned-soldier. Even when he had a say in his life's path, he was rarely permitted to access his voice and make any real choice for himself." Bodhi crosses the room slowly and sits on the couch, angling his left ankle over his right knee as he dons a thoughtful expression. "Connery was the right hand of the king. Held the king's most guarded secrets. Carried out his most gruesome deeds."

Connery turns his head away from me and buries it under the couch again.

I see the movement for the shame it is. I can't help myself. My hand runs over his gray and brown fur, soothing his angst as best I am able.

Bodhi's voice is quiet, even as Jonathan carries Seven closer, lowering her feet so she can scamper to Connery's other side and throw her small body over his massive frame.

Such an empath.

Bodhi watches us while he explains the things I am reluctant to believe. "Connery has more blood on his hands than just about anyone in our world. The king's mage stole Connery's will at the first available moment of newly minted adulthood, and that's how he's been for more than twenty years. The best kind of soldier is one who can't hesitate to carry out the king's command."

Only the way Bodhi says it all, "soldier" could be replaced with the more derogatory "dog."

"Connery tracked down everyone who came down with the disease. Only loyalty to the throne matters to the king, and the disease marks you as disloyal."

Connery cries. There's no other word for it. His big body trembles and a barely audible whimper escapes him.

"Stop it!" I glare up at Bodhi. "Can't you see your story is upsetting him?"

Bodhi smiles down at me as if I am a child. "Ah, but my story isn't over. Of all the luck in the world, Connery's very best friend is arrested." He motions to his ankle tracker, then addresses Jonathan's withering stare. "What, you don't think a shifter and a mage can be friends?"

Jonathan's nose crinkles. "No, I find it hard to believe you have friends at all."

Bodhi chuckles at the clever dig. "Touché. We're an odd pairing, to be sure."

Jonathan and I snort in unison.

Seven pipes in, keeping up with the conversation I can barely comprehend. "You've got the disease, too?"

Bodhi extends his hand and boops her on the nose affectionately. "Yes, sweet girl. The king himself found my lesions, so my incarceration was inevitable." He shrugs as if his trauma is to be expected.

Seven's shoulders deflate. "That's very sad."

Bodhi shrugs. "Hazards of being orphaned and having your life assigned to you without your consent."

Seven kneels on Connery's other side, stroking his fur. "I'm orphaned, too."

Connery pulls his head out from under the couch and stares at me quizzically.

I run my tongue along my top row of teeth before answering. "My sister gave birth to Seven. When she died, I adopted her." I state the whole ordeal as if it doesn't gut me on a regular basis that I am nowhere near the kind of mother Aashya was.

Bodhi regards Seven in a new light. "Then we have something in common, sweet girl." All levity leaves Bodhi as he continues. "The most loyal man to the throne contracted the disease only enemies of the throne can get. When you left Crimshade, Connery, I was sent to Common to hunt you down and bring you back, so they can mount your head on the wall and bury your freewill where the rest of our pride has been discarded. If there's one thing King Artifice hates more than disloyalty, it's being wrong. He was wrong when he thought he would always be able to control you. The king won't stop until you pay for proving him wrong."

My mouth dries as my hand stills in Connery's fur. Whatever I thought I was getting into when I took this stray into my home, I had no idea it would lead to this.

9

TRAITOR'S DISEASE

I don't know if I am still in denial or if I am enraged that a world exists that would classify a disease as a show of someone's character.

I'd hoped we were past that as a society, but I guess ignorance is not limited to earth.

Or Common, as they call it.

Connery's nostrils flare. He inhales as if smelling an invisible flower. *"No one's here now. No soldiers. Tha's good."*

I point to Bodhi's ankle from my spot beside Connery on the living room floor. "But they're coming, right? These people who put a tracker on you, they're on their way because you led them here. Soldiers." I purse my lips, my hand stilling over Connery's back. "Is this your revenge on Connery for doing things he couldn't control? You're leading the soldiers to him? Why else would you be here?"

Bodhi scoffs at me, his feathers ruffled. "Revenge is for small minds, and I assure you, there is nothing small about me." He sends a smirk in Jonathan's direction, then turns back to me. "No, poppet, I'm not about to lead anyone here. I want to get Connery to safety, so he can die in peace."

"Die? That's not going to happen. I fixed his arm!" I fret, my tone climbing to panic.

Seven's voice matches mine. "No, Connery! You can't die! I love you!" Without hesitation, Seven bursts into tears, laying her body over Connery's while she weeps.

I have to remind myself that she is seven, and her reaction is appropriate. I am thirty-three, so throwing myself over my dog's body and weeping dramatically is not.

At least, not when there are witnesses.

Jonathan narrows his eyes at Bodhi. "See what you did there?"

Bodhi looks on Seven's tears and my creeping anxiety with discomfort bordering disdain. "Stop that," he scolds us, as if shooing away a fart.

Jonathan crosses his arms over his chest. "Fix it."

Bodhi rolls his eyes and then kneels beside Seven, checking his trousers to make sure no floor dust soils the fabric. "There, there... child."

"Seven," she informs him.

"That's a horrible name for a lovely girl. That won't do. No, no. You'll be Petunia. That's a lovely flower."

My upper lip curls at him. "Her name is what she says it is, jackass." I straighten. "Which is a word we don't use."

Bodhi reaches into his shirt sleeve and pulls out a perfect pink petunia with all the flourish of a magic trick, then hands it to Seven. "There you go. Just for you."

Seven sniffles as she takes the flower, but her other hand remains on her dog. "How do we fix Connery? Is there medicine? I have Band-Aids. They're pink and glittery."

Bodhi shakes his head. "Not that I know of. It's incurable." He unbuttons his cuff and shows his forearm to Seven and to me. "See this?"

He has flawless skin on his hands, face, and neck, but his forearm looks like it has been ravaged by boils, or perhaps a rash that has gone horribly wrong.

Seven gasps while I recoil. "Is it catchy? Is it scratchy?"

Bodhi smirks at her phrasing. "It's very scratchy, yes. It's not contagious, no. It just happens as people go about their normal lives in our world. It'll get worse, until chunks of my skin fall clean off and never grow back. One day in the future, the lesions will move inside my body, and I won't be able to breathe. Then I will die."

He says it all matter-of-factly, explaining the ways of the world to her without emotion or sugarcoating.

Seven reaches out her hand that holds the flower so she can wrap her arm around Bodhi's neck.

It is clear Bodhi has never been this close to a child

before because his body goes rigid, even as he acquiesces to Seven's pull. "I don't want you to die."

He blinks through the emotion that I can tell is beginning to crack through his stoic demeanor. "I don't either, but that's the way of it sometimes."

Resolve drapes over me like a steel vest, protecting me from the ugly nature of the truth. "No. Connery lives here, and he's not dying. I'll take him to the vet, and he'll be fixed. That's that."

Bodhi quirks an eyebrow at my defiance. "Is that so? All our magic did nothing, but you think a normal human can solve it all?"

My upper lip curls. "I think Connery belongs here, so I'm going to take care of him."

And just like that, I stand, deciding on the fly that this is the thing that is going to happen.

I ignore Bodhi. I ignore Seven's weeping. I don't even listen to the loud look of warning Jonathan casts my way.

I search for the nearest vet on my phone and then grab up my keys.

I call sharply to Connery, who finally takes his head out from under the couch. "Let's go, Connery. I'm taking you to the vet. If your world can't heal you, mine will."

Bodhi stands, fixing me with a resigned sigh, looking unruffled and picture perfect even after kneeling on the floor. "You can't even cure the common cold."

I snarl at him. "You don't know what I can do."

Connery follows as I stomp out of the house, with Seven and Jonathan on my heels and fire in my veins.

I will not let my dog die. Not when I barely understand what's going on and this stranger tells me there is no other option.

I may not be able to advocate for myself at work, asking for the raise I know I deserve. But if someone so much as looks at Seven the wrong way, I won't hesitate to move heaven and earth to rectify the situation. This other world Bodhi speaks about locks up people who are sick?

No. I won't stand for anyone hurting my dog like that. I won't let him die just because this ridiculously insecure king says he must.

Seven loves this dog. I brought Connery into this house. It's my responsibility to deal with the situation now.

I shove my feet into my shoes. "Connery, let's go."

Connery comes like a good boy, his head down as if he's expecting me to kick him out.

I hate that I ordered him like a dog, and that he obeyed as such. I stop and turn toward him. "I'm sorry. I shouldn't have bossed you like that."

Connery regards me with his head tilted to the side, as if no one has ever apologized to him.

That only makes me angrier.

I hand Seven her white straw hat with the daisy on it— her fashionable attire for going outside, even when it's a Midwest winter out. "Let's go, babe."

Jonathan shoots me a wary look but doesn't otherwise argue. I know what he's thinking: digging my heels in deeper is only going to make things worse in the long run.

Connery isn't mine. I should let him go with Bodhi and let fate do its thing.

If only I didn't have this stubborn streak and a soft spot for strays.

10

VISIT TO THE VET

I grit my teeth and pretend nothing is scary at all as I march to my green sedan, open the passenger door for Connery and help him up, then wait for the others to pile in. "Jonathan, can you sit with Seven, just in case? I don't want her back there with Bodhi by herself."

Bodhi straightens. "I'm fairly certain I'm to be offended by that."

I shove the keys in the ignition. "Then be offended. I don't know you, man."

Jonathan doesn't even blink. "Absolutely. Sit with the princess? My privilege." He squeezes his taller, firmer body into the back beside Seven's booster seat. "Can I borrow your hat for a few, Seven? I think it would look good with my outfit."

Seven indulges him in a bit of dress-up while Bodhi

opens the passenger's side door expectantly. "To the back with you, Connery," he commands without asking politely.

My upper lip curls. "Connery, stay right where you are. Bodhi, you're relegated to the backseat. My car, my dog, my rules."

Bodhi shoots me a withering stare, as if he cannot believe I would deign to send him to a place of less privilege. "You do realize I'm a mage. That should mean something, even in Common."

I roll my eyes and turn on the engine. "You do realize I don't care. Your awesome carnival tricks mean nothing to me if you can't heal my dog. Time for actual, non-magical magic called modern medicine." I jerk my thumb over my shoulder. "Backseat."

Bodhi mutters under his breath as he complies. While he is leaner than Jonathan, his lanky body still takes up enough space to make it an effort to cram himself into the back.

I smile wickedly, glad Bodhi is uncomfortable.

"Why don't you just sit on my lap?" Bodhi says crossly.

Jonathan squirms in the middle seat. "Where do you want me to move? I'm just as squished as you."

"Doubtful. If we just throw the booster seat out the window, we'll have more room."

"She's seven years old. She needs a booster seat until she turns eight," I rule, going by the book in all things parenting, just so I don't miss something that turns out to be important.

Connery sits without complaint as we drive to the nearest veterinary office, listening to Seven sing a silly song she learned at school about donuts and counting. I'm not totally sure, since she only ever sings the first half over and over.

When we get there, mercifully, they have an opening for us and not much wait time. The waiting room smells like rubbing alcohol and loads of animal hair. Seven holds her nose delicately while we take up most of the seats.

Connery sniffs the air, does a lap of the four corners of the waiting room, and then plops himself beside me like a gargoyle, intimidating enough to fend off anything that comes near me. When he deems there is no immediate threat, Connery rests his massive head on my thigh. My hand finds its way to his ears, rubbing the soft felt between my fingers just to watch his eyelids droop contentedly. I lean down and kiss the top of his head. "Don't you worry, sweetheart. The vet will fix you right up."

Connery doesn't answer. I get the feeling he's humoring me with this trip to the vet.

I didn't even ask him if he wanted to go, or if it was okay to give this a try. Sometimes I do that—bowl people over in my quest to do what I believe needs to be done.

Regret washes over me. "I did it again," I admit to him as I get off my chair and kneel on the floor that has dog slobber and who knows what else on it, making it slightly sticky. "I made it all about my agenda, and not you. Sometimes I get like this," I admit sheepishly. "I get all amped up about something, get super passionate, and then act without discussing it with the people affected. I didn't even ask you if you wanted to go here. I'm sorry, Connery. I was so mad at your terrible king; I didn't think."

Connery blinks at me with those beautiful blue eyes. When he answers, he keeps his voice low so the receptionist doesn't overhear. *"You're apologizing to me?"* He says it as if no one has ever done that to him in his life.

I nod slowly. "Better late than never. Is it okay that I took you here? They're going to examine you and look at your leg to see what they can do to help."

Connery licks my cheek. *"There is nothing anyone can do to help, but I understand ye have to figure tha out for yourself."* He rests his maw on my shoulder so I can wrap my arms around his fat neck. I don't like hugs normally, but apparently my daughter and my dog are the two loopholes to that hard and fast part of my occasionally prickly personality. *"No matter how hard ye resist it, I am dying."*

My eyes squeeze shut. "Don't say that. We just found each other." The little girl in me still believes in fate, in meant to be.

In happy endings.

Huh. I really thought that part of me was buried with my sister's remains.

"Should you even be with us?" Jonathan asks quietly, elbowing Bodhi, who is encroaching on his personal space without regard for anyone else. "Won't that tracker lead the people who want to capture Connery right to us?"

Bodhi rolls his eyes as if the whole issue is beneath him. "Do you really know nothing of mages?"

Jonathan's eyes widen at Bodhi's rudeness. My best friend moves his hand in a circle around Bodhi's visage. "Mages are fictional! So no, I don't know anything about what you say you are. Explain it or go away, so you don't lead drama right to us." He points at me and then at Seven. "These two ladies are the only two constants in my life. I don't play fast and loose with their safety."

I purse my lips at the shielding statement. I debate saying something to deflect it because I don't like the over-protective man vibe that sometimes comes out. I don't need protecting. Never have. But I let Jonathan have this one, since I know it comes from a good place.

Bodhi crosses his arms, and I watch Seven mirror his movements from her seat on Jonathan's other side. "Rule number one: you'll never know all that mages can do because we don't like to be known. So I'm not giving you a detailed list of how useful and brilliant I am. Not even my people know all there is to know about mages. We have evolving magic. Meaning nature can create new abilities as needed over time."

Jonathan softens his attitude marginally, leaning his head back against the white wall that has pictures of puppies sporadically placed in between giant blown up portraits of fleas to advertise protecting your animals. "Evolving magic? That's pretty cool."

Bodhi quiets. "But then as soon as that new ability is known, people want unfettered access to it. They want their problems solved by mages instead of muddling through on their own. And the evolution is slow, sometimes taking lifetimes to move the needle an inch. Magic potency and nuance vary from mage to mage, so we mostly keep our specific abilities to ourselves. Plus there aren't all that many of us left."

Seven stands on her toes and moves to Bodhi, clasping her hands under her pointed chin. "If you tell me your secret powers, I promise not to tell anyone!"

Bodhi smiles at her cuteness. "Oh, dear Petunia, the best secrets are the ones no one gets to hear. Then we can imagine my abilities are far more impressive than they actually are."

Her little mouth screws to the side. "Is that your fancy way of telling me to mind my own business?"

Bodhi chuckles. "I suppose it is."

Jonathan scrubs his hand over his face. "Thanks for the education, but my original point was that you shouldn't be here because whoever is hunting Connery is going to be led straight to him because of that tracker you're wearing. If he's really your friend and you really didn't come here to bring him back to the people who were abusing him, then you wouldn't have come here. You would have led them away from him."

Bodhi's lips purse, and even though my attention is diverted as I fill out the paperwork while we wait for the doctor to be available, I can tell even offering a small explanation of his powers pains him.

"When I was incarcerated, as all citizens in Crimshade are once we contract the disease—we're too valuable to be locked away and forgotten, as the rest of the people are—there was a mage in my cell with me. Miro. One of his abilities is to..." Bodhi looks from left to right, making sure no one else hears. "Miro can dull certain magical objects until they lose all usefulness. Of course, the authorities don't know that. But when he learned that I would be let out for a span of time to locate Connery, he spelled my tracker. It was working at full force for a while, but the signal grows weaker by the minute, and I wasted a fair bit of time on purpose trying to locate Connery. I stayed for two nights in a rat-infested abandoned house so they would tear the place apart looking for him there. The signal is weaker now. I'm hoping too weak for them to follow, but I can't be sure. Magic isn't always a science."

Jonathan's shoulders deflate in time with mine. That factor has been of no small concern.

When the vet is ready to see us, I carry Connery into the small examination room. He's heavy, that's for sure, but I'm thinking he shouldn't be putting weight on his wounded leg. He could limp there, but my heart can't take it.

Jonathan offers to carry him for me, but I shake my head. "No, no. I've got him."

I frown at Bodhi's chuckle that hits my ears. "Never thought I'd see the day. Good for you, Connery. You're learning to lean on someone. Granted, it's because you have no choice in the matter, but still. Quite the transformation."

Connery grumbles not ungratefully to me. *"Ye don't have to do this, ye know. I'm not a toddler, and I wasn't carried like this even when I was."*

I kiss the side of his furry face as my muscles groan under his weight. "I know you're not. Please let me. You're my sweetie pie, and you're injured. Let me baby you a little bit until you're back on your feet."

He rests his head on my shoulder, but I can hear errant murmuring of confusion in his mind. *"Why are ye being nice to me?"*

The question stops me cold. Even though I ache to put him down, I turn my chin enough so he can see how serious I am when I answer. "Families take care of each other. You're living under my roof, so I'm going to look after you. This is what that looks like."

He marvels at the notion as if it's the strangest thing he's ever heard, which is even more heartbreaking.

I set Connery atop the cold metal table in the tiny exam room as we all pile in, with Seven on Jonathan's hip. I can tell Connery is nervous at being near the vet, so I keep my arm under his neck so he can rest his head in the crook of my elbow. I run my fingers over his fur while I answer the vet's perfunctory questions.

When the vet is focused on Connery's leg, I vocalize that I want more than a brace. "Can we get a full blood panel done?" I try to fish for a reason a vet would believe. "He's been a little green around the gills, and I want to make sure he's alright. This leg is infected, and I'm curious how that happened and what it is we're dealing with."

The vet's lips purse as she stares me down. "You realize this isn't a dog, right? I should be calling Animal Control."

Bodhi takes a step forward, locking eyes with the vet. "It's a dog, and I believe the lady of the house asked for bloodwork. And put a rush on it. This is the most important task of your day." He meets Connery's gaze with a certainty that communicates Connery will never be on his own again.

I don't expect Bodhi's pushiness to get us anywhere, so when the veterinarian complies with a glassy, unfocused look to her, I take a step back.

Jonathan frowns at Bodhi and whispers to him unhappily. "What did you just do?"

But Bodhi can't access words just yet. A swoon takes him over, so Jonathan and I scramble to catch him before his tall body hits the ground while Connery barks an alert.

We lower him into the only chair in the room while Seven fans him with her decorative hat.

The veterinarian does her work as if she and Connery are the only ones in the small, square room. She moves as if in a trance, taking Connery's blood, checking vitals and administering something in a vial.

"What is that?" I ask before she injects the needle.

She rattles off a chemical compound and then informs me with a monotoned, "Vitamin shot. He's sallow and needs a boost."

I look to Connery, who gives me a brief nod of consent.

"That's fine," I tell her, then turn my head back to Bodhi, who doesn't look all that coherent. "Is he alright, Jonathan?"

My best friend shoots me a harried scowl. "Do I look like I know what I'm doing? I'm an ad rep, not a doctor!"

Seven scampers to Connery's side and holds his paw while the vet administers the shot. She squeals her angst because shots are the big trauma of a child's doctor visit. "It's okay, sweet boy! I'm here for you. I love you so much. Just breathe through it. Don't look! Don't look! Oo, it's really gross."

I try not to laugh. I mean, really, not much about this day has been funny, but Seven's reaction to Connery getting a shot is too adorable to let me cling to my fear alone.

"Seven, Connery is okay. He's a big boy."

Connery's voice has been silent in the company of the doctor, but at Seven's doting, he offers a gentle, *"Love."*

I know he means he loves Seven's little heart, and perhaps that he feels her love because she doesn't hold it back like a hand of poker she doesn't want you to see. She wears her love proudly and boldly, daring the world to tell her it's wrong or not enough.

I am only like that for her. And Jonathan. And now Connery, apparently. I love her without limits or reason, and I wouldn't have it any other way.

Seven places her hat over Connery's face to shield him from the awful sight of the work the vet must do.

The vet examines every bit of his fur, noting a few patches that have a skin abnormality underneath. "Curious," she comments.

"Can you take scrapings if you don't know what it is?"

"I mean, I know what it is, but I've only seen this sort of thing in textbooks. Never on an animal."

I lean forward, holding Connery protectively. "What is it?"

She steps back, her brows pinched. "This animal has contracted leprosy. It's small right now, but without antibiotics, it will spread and eventually kill him."

Seven squeaks her distress. "Not my baby-baby!"

Jonathan frowns from his spot beside Bodhi, making sure the mage stays propped up in his seat. "You mean like Biblical leprosy? Like, actual leprosy?" He takes a step forward but still holds onto Bodhi's shoulder. "There has to be a cure, right? I mean, leprosy isn't a thing anymore, but it used to be."

The veterinarian nods. "Connery will need to be on steroids for the inflammation, and also antibiotics. I can administer them today, if you like. A couple months for everything to go away for good is worst-case scenario, but I think he'll be chasing squirrels far sooner than that. I would imagine he'll be right as rain in a week or two."

Bodhi sags in his chair. "Leprosy? What is that?"

The veterinarian gives a slightly more clinical explanation than I can muster. "It's an infection. That's the short version. The longer version is that it's a disease that eats away at the skin, leaving lesions until a limb is either rendered useless or completely severed. It can be contagious if you're not careful. I would recommend the four of you going on antibiotics for just one week to make sure you didn't contract anything when you came into contact with this dog."

Every time the veterinarian says "dog," her nose twitches, as if she knows Connery is a wolf, but her mind has a veil over it that keeps the facts at bay.

My heart races. If I brought a disease into our home and Seven gets sick because of it?

I know our next stop needs to be a doctor.

The vet performs an x-ray on Connery's front paw and rules it is not broken, but it would get stronger faster with a brace. Jonathan takes Seven out into the waiting room for the whole thing. Connery assures me that I don't need to hover, but it's a nonnegotiable. "You're part of the family now. You don't suffer alone ever again. That's the rule of the house."

Medicine is administered and prescribed. Connery is given a complete physical exam. Everything that can be done for him, including being prescribed a multivitamin to make sure he heals swiftly, is done while Bodhi struggles to remain upright in his seat.

Whatever Bodhi did to the vet, making her believe Connery wasn't a wolf, took a lot out of him. His complexion is sallow, his movements sluggish instead of graceful. Though, he still has that haughty look in his lavender eyes, so I'm guessing he'll be just fine in time. If he was compliant, then I'd really start to worry.

I fill my purse with Connery's meds, paying nearly a week's salary to the receptionist when I check out.

Connery limps by my side because I cannot carry him as I want to do. I have to support Bodhi, who is walking like a drunk that's been shot in the leg.

Somehow we make it to the car, but instead of going home, I know exactly where I need to drive next.

11

BODHI AND CONNERY

Jonathan treats us all to fruit smoothies at his favorite overpriced juice bar that (thankfully) allows dogs in the patio area out back.

"What kind would you like?" I ask Connery, kneeling beside him after the others place their orders. I know Connery won't want to talk aloud, so I get close so he can whisper his preference in my ear.

"*Ye don't have to worry about me. Whatever ye get me is grand.*"

I frown at him, rubbing the silk of his ears. "No, babe. You're a person here. You matter. You're allowed a voice. You get to have opinions and I want to hear them. I want to know you."

Connery regards me with confusion mingled with wonder, as if no one has said that to him in a very long time.

Which makes sense, since he's been enslaved without his will intact for... wow, for twenty-two years. He probably has no idea how to make decisions like this.

I soften at the conundrum. "Let's look at the menu together. What sounds good to you?"

Connery leans his cheek to mine while I kneel on the icy pavement at the order window, ignoring the impatience of the clerk. I stroke his maw, keeping his face pressed to mine. *"I don't know what some of these flavors are. We have different food than ye do here, I think. We've been on the edge of famine for a long time. Tastes aren't really a priority where I'm from."*

I swallow down that hard truth. "Then the real question is: do you want to try something familiar or something new?"

He licks my fingers. *"It's wrong to ask ye for anything. You've been so good to me already."*

It's then that I reach for the logic I've infused into Seven over and over again. "You're allowed to take up space in the world. It's okay to be who you are, and it's okay not to have all the answers just yet. We're all figuring out our lives."

I love massaging his jowls. He leans into my touch as if he can't get enough, which suits me just fine. *"What's passionfruit? Is tha something I can choose?"*

My grin cannot be helped as I stand, kissing him atop his head before I address the clerk. "A passionfruit smoothie bowl, please. Can you add protein powder to it?"

While they assemble our order, I stroke his fur lovingly. "That was good, Connery."

Bodhi watches the exchange through lidded eyes, a tender expression crossing his features until we join him at the patio table with sugary smoothies. After ten minutes of Bodhi slurping his drink, finally he has some color back in his cheeks.

Jonathan speaks gently to Bodhi, donning his best company manners because he's a softy when someone isn't feeling well.

"I'll be alright," Bodhi assures us as we sit at the picnic table on the side of the restaurant, shivering in our jackets. "Mages used to be more adept at mind warping, but the magic's been fading for decades. I only possess a cursory knowledge of the skill, and the people of Crimshade can easily deflect that sort of thing. Fortunately, Common isn't educated in fending off a mage's influence. I took a chance, and thankfully it worked. I didn't want the veterinarian getting anyone else involved." He takes another long pull of his drink while Seven hums to herself, her legs dangling on the bench beside me.

Bodhi's eyes are hollow with purple rings beneath to match his lavender irises. "Do you think she's right? Do you think your medicine might actually... Do you think it can cure the traitor's disease?"

My head bobs. "I think we'll have to wait and see. But if it truly is leprosy, we have cures for that. It'll just take time for the medicine to do its thing."

"I want the medicine," Bodhi rules, determination flaring even though he looks as sturdy as a feather. "I need it."

Seven chimes in. "You can have some of mine! It tastes like bubble gum. Super yummy."

My free hand moves through her hair. "Not that kind of medicine, baby. As soon as you're feeling up to it, we're all going to Urgent Care to get on antibiotics. That should clear you up just fine, Bodhi. You'll probably need steroids for your inflammation, but it's all solvable."

Bodhi's eyes water as he stares at me, drinking in my words as if they are the first glimmer of hope that's quenched his parched soul. "My people are dying. Slowly and with painful disfigurements. I'd made my peace with the idea of going out the same way. Now you're telling me it's as simple as seeing one of your doctors? I could be healed in a week or two?"

Jonathan nods from his spot beside Bodhi. "Medicine is our version of magic. We'll help you as best we can, Bodhi."

Bodhi rears back at Jonathan's promise. His mouth sours as he digests the kindness as if it's a foreign, bitter herb. "No one helps me. I have a disease. Once you contract it, your friends and family desert you, even though you swear you haven't been disloyal to the throne. You have no one, and the people you thought were yours become the king's. They turn you in to him and away you go to rot in a windowless prison with the others who have no idea how they got there. Granted, the only friends I had left were the ones in the brothel where I was rented out, but still, it stung to have them turn on me like that."

"Brothel?" Jonathan questions.

Bodhi nods slowly. "When you age out of the orphanage, you're designated for either the brothel or serving in the king's army. Felix, Fritz, and Connery have builds far more suited for combat than me, so when I became an adult, I was taken from them—the only family I'd ever known—and thrown to the greedy hands of men who should have known better." He motions to the three of us. "And you say you're going to help me? You don't even know me. Maybe I am disloyal to the king."

Seven takes a break from slurping. "What's a brothel?"

I glower at Bodhi, even though part of me wants to hold his hand while he unburdens himself of the details of what sounds like a very difficult life. There is far more to his world than I was prepared to handle. But I know that when someone has been through a trauma, the best thing to do is listen.

Then get revenge on whoever caused such terrible pain.

One thing at a time. Listening first.

Bodhi's hand runs over Seven's hair. "It's a sad, lonely place, Petunia. It's where you become a mere toy to be passed around with no thought to your safety or longevity. It's where you go when you have no one who cares where you are."

Connery gives a derisive bark. *"I cared, Bodhi. I just... I couldn't get to ye."*

Bodhi inclines his head to his friend. "I misspoke. I know you would have come for me if you could. Felix and Fritz, too. And I would have come for you sooner if that were an option. That's why I jumped at the chance to track you down when I learned you'd escaped the king's mage." He offers Connery a wan smile. "We did it. We're out of the orphanage and finally back together." His smile turns wicked. "They're going to rue the day they didn't kill us both."

A low growl rumbles in Connery's throat after he takes a lick of his smoothie bowl on the ground. *"When I go back, I will tear out the king's throat for what he did to ye."*

I blink at the two, trying to keep up.

Bodhi sips his smoothie. "Funny. I was going to do the same to him for what he did to you. Whoever gets there first wins."

Connery yips in agreement.

They're going to have to beat me there if they want to take down the king. While I've never murdered a soul, the urge to avenge them both is strong.

Seven chimes in, asking the thing I want to say, but I'm too polite to voice it. "What did the king do to you?"

Bodhi fiddles with his straw when Connery goes mute. "The king ordered his mage to take away Connery's ability to think or speak or act for himself. He made him his slave, which is unforgivable for one being to do to another." He takes another drink of his smoothie. "Then the king took me. He feels entitled to treat himself to the spoils of the land he rules with an iron fist and a flaccid..." He pauses, censoring himself, thank goodness. "King Artifice made me his toy for quite some time. Whenever I tried to escape, he ordered Connery to bring me back to his chambers."

Connery lowers his head in shame, though I can tell Bodhi doesn't hold him responsible in the slightest.

I shiver and motion to Seven's drink, wishing there was anything I could do or say to unmake that horrible part of their history. "Finish your smoothie, honey." Then to Bodhi, I say, "You're going to stay with us. Understood?"

Bodhi softens at my offer that comes out like a command. "Harboring a fugitive is a punishable offense."

"Then I should probably harbor two fugitives and really roll the dice. It's done, Bodhi. You're staying with me. Both of you. Give you a chance to breathe."

Jonathan's mouth tightens. I can tell he is digesting all the social stigma he's had to deal with when he found out he was HIV positive. He lost a great many friends in one fell swoop. He clutches his smoothie cup, his words coming out more forceful than gentle. "Diseases are nature's fault, not ours. Being loyal to your ruler doesn't make you a good person or a bad one. It means you're a person with opinions." He stares at his straw, a hollow look coming over him. "Nature can do some pretty cruel things, kicking you when you're already down and destined to be alone. Sometimes natures pushes you further out to sea." Then he snaps marginally out of his sadness, turning his chin to Bodhi. "We won't let you drown."

Bodhi lowers his chin, true humility overtaking his brash confidence. "However I can use my magic to help you, I will. You took in my best friend and got him your medicine. You haven't kicked me out, even though you know I have the traitor's disease. And now you're going to help me get the cure and give me a place to sleep?" Bodhi shakes his head. "There are far better people than me who deserve this medicine a lot more than I do. People who matter, who spoke aloud against the king and were punished severely for it. Unfortunately, medicine doesn't cure the dead."

I reach across the table and rest my chilly hand atop his. I note the jolt in his body language, the shock over a person willingly making physical contact with him.

Jonathan was like that for a while when he was first diagnosed and lost most of the people in his life. I spent a fair amount of time holding my best friend while he wept on my couch, telling me I shouldn't be near him because he's diseased and dirty—neither of which have ever been true.

I snap my fingers to garner Jonathan's attention. "Hey, I love you. Do you hear me?"

Jonathan locks his gaze on mine, tethering himself to

my strong will when he is in danger of drifting off to his land of despair.

Finally, he bobs his head at me. "I love you, too."

I curl my fingers around Bodhi's hand, voicing a promise I shouldn't make aloud. "After you're cured, we'll get a super-sized stock of medicine that you can take back to your people. They deserve a cure. They deserve to have all their limbs and strength so they can stand against this dictator who tells them how terrible they are without bothering to learn who they are."

A tear cascades down Bodhi's cheek, setting Seven loose. She pops up from her spot and races around Connery, who is still drinking his smoothie from a bowl on the ground beside me. She throws her dainty arms around Bodhi's neck, doing her best to rock him from side to side because she cannot stand it when anyone is crying.

She weeps along with him, though I'm sure she only partly understands the depths of the damage Bodhi has endured.

My little empath. Her heart breaks over and over for others, yet she remains strong and unbreakable when she is deserted.

Like mother, like daughter, I suppose.

"I'll have a talk with the people in your world," Seven assures him. "I'll make them see that you're my sweetie pie. Connery too. They just don't know how to be nice. I'll teach them." She kisses Bodhi's cheek and then thumbs away his tears as they fall.

Damn this sweetness. I'm on the verge of crying myself, watching her love this stranger so wholly.

Bodhi manages a small smile for her. "You'd do that for me?"

Seven nods with fierce determination in her big brown eyes. "When people thought I was a boy, I was sad all the time. Now that I'm a girl, I lost a lot of friends, too. But they just need time to grow up. To learn that they're not always right, and that no one should control someone else's future."

I hear my sister's words and mine coming out of her mouth, sending a tingle down my spine.

Seven squeezes his neck tighter. "Everyone is learning how to be kind. Some people are just smarter than others at kindness. But I'm a great teacher, Bodhi. I'll talk to your people and make them see that you're a good boy."

Bodhi is a mix of amusement and depression, both of which come out of him in the form of more tears. He does his best attempt at a smile, directing it only at Seven. "I do believe that if the world would educate themselves on the job of kindness, neither of our hearts would be this broken. I adore you, my little Petunia."

She leans into him, hugging him as they rock from side to side.

Finally, Bodhi's arms wrap around her. His eyes close while my heart threatens to swell and break at the sight of this sweet child leading the way into the future with kindness as her shield and hugs as her weapon.

12

TAKING CARE OF EACH OTHER

By the time we get through Urgent Care and the pharmacy, I feel as if I could sleep a solid eight hours smack in the middle of the day.

The aim is to grab two pizzas and try to keep up with Seven's bubbly energy until nightfall.

Emotions make me sleepy if I get too near them, and she's been running high on the stuff for hours. We all have.

Seven won't let Connery out of her sight, insisting he eat beside her so she can use one hand to munch on her pizza and the other to pet him. Jonathan and Bodhi are making polite chitchat when she looks around the table and tears up, her pointed chin quivering.

"Baby girl, what's wrong?" I ask her, setting down my crust.

"This is the first time we've had all four chairs used at

dinner. There's always at least one chair empty. Now we have a big family, like I always wanted." She points to a tear on her cheek. "This isn't a sadness tear. My heart's too full of happiness to keep them inside, so they squeezed out of me."

Now I'm getting choked up. "I didn't realize you wanted a bigger family."

She shrugs, as if it should be obvious that that's what she's been craving all along. "Sure. Now I have a mommy, a daddy, a big brother and a dog."

Connery barks once to let her know he is fully onboard with fulfilling her wish.

Bodhi spears his salad. "Which one am I?"

Jonathan answers "the dog" at the same time Seven replies with a cheery, "My brother!"

Jonathan smirks at Bodhi's indignation shock while he eats.

As evening turns to night, Jonathan and I move through the motions of getting Seven ready for bed. Bodhi keeps checking the windows, making sure no one is coming for Connery, while my sweet dog sniffs the four corners of the house.

In the back of my brain, I know that Connery is not a dog. I know he's not even fully a wolf. But I can't grasp a concept like magic in real life just yet, so for now, he's the dog I've always wanted.

After I read Seven another chapter of Roald Dahl's *Matilda* for the millionth night in a row and sing the bedtime song twice, I am looking forward to sleeping in my bed beside my new dog.

When I come down the stairs, I catch a few notes of the exchange between Jonathan and Bodhi. "I'll sleep on the couch," Bodhi tells him.

"No, you'll sleep on the floor."

Bodhi's face pulls. "Is there a reason I can't have even the barest amount of comfort? You all preach acceptance and that the disease wasn't my fault but rather nature's, yet I'm not good enough to sleep on the couch?"

Jonathan crosses his arms over his chest. "I sleep on the couch. That's my spot whenever I stay over. You sleep on the floor."

Bodhi motions to the hallway where my bedroom lies. "I would think a man might sleep with his wife and leave the couch to the guest."

Now it's Jonathan's turn to blanche.

Gee, thanks.

"Zara is not my wife. She's my best friend. I'm gay."

I can tell this information makes Bodhi pleased.

Bodhi's mouth falls open as the world rights itself again for him. "Ah, that makes more sense. Very well, then I'll flip you for the couch."

I do a poor job of holding back the amusement from my tone. "Jonathan gets the couch because that's where he always sleeps when he stays over. Bodhi, I'll get a stack of blankets so thick for you, you'll swear you're sleeping on a cloud."

Bodhi meets my eyes with a hollow gaze, all levity deserting him. "I'm used to sleeping on concrete, since a mage's cell is bereft of anything that might be manipulated by our magic." Then he shoots Jonathan an inquiring look. "Really? That didn't move you to give me the couch?"

Jonathan flops on the cushions, sprawling out just to be a jerk. "Nope."

I chuckle to myself as I pull out all the blankets we have and lay them on the floor in a tall stack for Bodhi. "A step up from the concrete floor of a prison cell, I'm sure." I let Connery out into the backyard, then I go to my bedroom and grab up two pairs of pajamas from the drawer I gave Jonathan, since he stays over often enough to need a supply of clean clothes. "There you go, boys." I lean down to kiss Jonathan's forehead. "Be nice."

"You're the one who needs that reminder usually, not me."

I smirk at him and then turn to Bodhi. While I don't know him well and I'm still not sure how I feel about having him in my house, it is physically impossible for me not to follow my normal routine and kiss everyone goodnight in my home.

I blame my sister for that one. She always insisted on affection. Hugs are too intimate for me, but a kiss on the forehead can be done without someone wrapping their arms around me like they're going to plunge me underwater and force me to feel things I don't want to go near.

I don't wait for awkwardness to overtake me. I close the

gap between myself and Bodhi, pecking his cheek in a manner that I hope communicates kindness and welcome.

Bodhi stiffens, his fingers moving to the spot of my affection on his face. "What is this? Why is this?"

I kiss his other cheek just to spite his attitude. "This is how we get married in my world. You're my husband now."

Bodhi steps back, a petrified look pulling at the corners of his mouth. "What?"

I laugh into my hand. "I'm kidding, Bodhi. I know I'm not your type."

It's my polite way of letting him know that I'm aware he's gay, and it's okay to be himself in my home.

Unless he's an absolute jag; then he can leave.

Bodhi wipes my kisses from his cheeks while Jonathan and I giggle together. "Hilarious. Goodnight, Zara. Your sense of humor needs a nap."

Jonathan gives me a fist-bump as I leave to let Connery back in.

As I wind down for the night with my dog by my side, I cannot believe how different our life has become in not even a week's time. Seven's right; we have a big family now.

"Do you want to sleep in the bed with me tonight?" I ask my dog.

Connery hesitates. *"Is tha okay?"*

I nod happily. "Of course. I just can't remember if I asked you last night or if I told you. Sorry if I didn't ask."

Connery tilts his head to the side, again perplexed that anyone asked his opinion.

I heft him up onto his side of the mattress, then I slide beneath the covers in my silk pajamas.

I stroke his fur as he rests his head on the pillow beside mine. "Long day," I confess through a yawn.

"Best day," Connery adds. *"My leg feels better than it did yesterday just from the vet cleaning it out. I tried passionfruit. I liked it."*

"I'm glad the vet was able to help you. I can't believe your king made you all think that a disease had anything to do with your loyalty, rather than that it's just an unfortunate malady. Super awful." I stroke the velvet of his ear, noting that he leans into my touch, his maw moving closer to my chin. I bury my face in the fur on his neck, my arms wrapping around his bulk because I love having a dog in my bed.

Connery is quiet a few beats before he whispers, *"Why are ye nice to me? Is this a game Commoners play? Is it going to end soon? Will ye be here in the morning, and will ye let me stay another day?"*

I kiss his face, my eyelids weighted. "You can stay forever. It's not a joke. It's not going to end." My words come out unpolished because of the late hour, or perhaps simply because it's easier to talk freely with a dog than it is people. "We belong together. Don't you feel it?"

Connery licks my cheek, drawing out a sleepy smile on my face. *"I've never felt anything like this."*

"It's going to be okay," I promise Connery. "I'll take care of you."

But as I say the words, I realize they aren't quite complete. He sticks tight to Seven's side whenever she needs him. He sniffs the house for predators.

I kiss his maw. "Maybe we'll take care of each other."

Connery sighs, licking my fingers to tell me he loves this plan.

My eyes close after a few more confessions, and finally, I drift off to sleep.

I don't expect Bodhi's voice to wake me not even an hour later, but his sharp whisper rouses me when Connery leaps off the bed. "Bodhi, what are you doing in here? Go back to sleep."

Bodhi rushes to my side of the bed, grabbing my hand and helping me to sit up. "We have to get out of here!"

"What?" I am marginally more awake now.

He holds my hand to his chest, his other hand on my back to steady me while I sway sitting up. "Quick! No lights, no talking above a whisper. If there's anything you absolutely need, grab it. Leave everything else. I'm getting us out of here."

Bodhi helps me out of the bed, holding onto my hand to guide me to my dresser.

"They've found us," he warns, the gravity in his tone waking me far faster than any cup of coffee ever could. "They're outside."

13

INTRUSION

odhi's arm falls around my frame. "I'll get you all out, but we have to move fast."

I can barely keep up. Connery is not even in the room anymore, taking Bodhi's words as a directive far quicker than I can snap to attention.

I manage to shove a sweater over my head and stuff my legs into jeans before Bodhi ushers me out of my bedroom. I collect my Instant Karma black hoodie and snatch up our winter coats and shoes. Bodhi guides me to the backdoor, where Jonathan is already dressed. He's standing with Seven in his arms, her head lolling on his shoulder.

Girlfriend can sleep through anything. I can only hope she holds no recollection of this intrusion.

Connery locks eyes with Bodhi, and I hear a clear

communication he sends out to all of us. *"The place is surrounded."*

Bodhi's mouth firms as I slide on my running shoes. "Very well. We're not done with this world, though. We need to bring back medicine."

Jonathan whispers, "I've got everyone's medicine." He unloops my purse from his arm and hands it to me. I hear the jingle of several pill bottles as my purse slides over my shoulder.

Bodhi motions for us to come closer, so we comply, huddling like we're playing a sport. "I can get us out of here, but it's going to take a lot out of me. I'll need to take you somewhere I can be incapacitated for a while. Do you know of anywhere like that?"

My tired brain struggles to keep up. "Won't they just track you down there?"

Bodhi shakes his head. "My tracker doesn't have any juice left in it. They must've caught the faint signal when I first came to you before it went out."

"My place," Jonathan rules. "You can crash there however long you need." Jonathan has never said that to a man, yet in this dire moment, his address spills out as I hear a rustling just outside.

"Did you hear that?" My whisper is pinched with worry.

Bodhi motions for us to gather even tighter to him. One arm falls around me and the other goes around

Jonathan and Seven, while Connery loops his tail around Bodhi's leg. "Hold tight to the child," Bodhi tells Jonathan.

My best friend clutches our sleeping girl tighter, casting me a firm, "Always."

More rustling outside, and I can tell we are just about out of time.

I close my eyes and lean into Bodhi's half-embrace. We are all so close together that I can tilt my chin and kiss the back of Seven's head.

It's the little things that connect me to her. The smell of her hair. The way she completely trusts Jonathan and me. The pink footie pajamas she is almost growing out of but refuses to surrender.

And now danger is at our doorstep.

My hand reaches up to shield the side of her face, should the soldiers bust in and come for us before Bodhi can get us out of here. Jonathan angles his shoulders to shield our princess with his body.

Appreciation wells in my soul for my best friend who stuck by me all through middle and high school, even though we were so very different. We were the only queer people in our classes, so we became each other's armor. Each other's soft place to land. He was the only out gay kid in the school, and I was the only bisexual brown girl anyone in our sheltered town had ever met.

Jonathan stuck by me even after graduation, when most friendships die off and go their separate ways. He moved in to look after me when my mother got sick, and then died not a month after her diagnosis.

He was at my house ten minutes after he got the call that my sister had passed.

He didn't try to talk me out of adopting Seven but did everything in his power to normalize her move into my condo.

Though I constantly worry he's outgrown me, Jonathan sticks by my side.

Even when I do foolish things like take in a stray wolf, thinking it's a dog.

Jonathan's always been the more gregarious of the two of us, making friends far easier. Yet he spends most evenings with us, playing house because he knows I have no idea what I'm doing but I'm too prideful to ask for help.

"I love you," I mouth to Jonathan.

He's a good man.

If I was a better woman, I would let him go, instead of tethering him to family life.

Bodhi holds us tighter, his eyes closing as someone outside fiddles with the doorknob, finding it locked.

I kick myself for not installing a security system.

From Bodhi's lips, a string of nonsense syllables spills out, filling the air with hope that perhaps we won't die for the crime of kindness.

I don't know how any of this works, but I cling to Bodhi and Jonathan, hoping that I didn't invite death to our doorstep while promising them a safe place to crash.

I hold my breath as a body slams into the backdoor. The urge to run out the front door with Seven is strong, but Connery already warned us that the house is surrounded.

Bodhi's body begins to tremble, not from fear, I don't think, but from strain. His torso is taut, and his arms begin to shake as more words I do not understand pour out of him. Even though there are no lights on, I can visualize the tension rolling off him. Bodhi's whispers turn up in volume as the kitchen window shatters, shocking a scream from me.

Seven stirs with a sleepy, "Mommy?"

Bodhi's arms tighten around us as his voice climbs to an incoherent shout.

A man's face appears in the broken window before he hurls a ball into my house.

I grip Jonathan's arm as he tugs my hood up over my head to protect me.

Neither of us knows what the weapon lobbed into my home might do.

Connery whines, clearly torn with indecision. Then suddenly he breaks from our huddle, limping toward the black sphere that looks like a shrunken bowling ball with twine coiled around it. He noses it into the living room and then races back to us, looping his tail around Bodhi's leg while Bodhi cries out in a pained voice.

An explosion from the living room shakes my bones,

rattling my teeth as part of my home shatters outward toward the street.

My home exploded. My home exploded. My home exploded.

Bodhi holds us together as he starts to sway, tethering my focus to keeping him upright rather than thinking about the damage to my home.

The backdoor splinters open with a handful of soldiers barreling toward us.

At the beginning of my scream, I see a man's face, his body clad in what looks like leather armor and a metal helmet, charging toward us with a legit sword in his fist.

At the end of my scream, I collapse in the center of Jonathan's home, terrified that the life I thought I knew is now no more.

14

JONATHAN'S HOUSEGUESTS

*B*eing transported ten miles in the span of a blink feels similar to riding a roller coaster, only it's paired with my bones being pulled nearly out of joint. We land in a pile of tangled limbs, though thankfully nothing feels broken.

"Why are we at Papa Jonathan's house?" Seven mumbles as she rights herself.

I shudder as my body figures itself out after I check Seven from head to toe that no injuries were sustained in the unorthodox trip.

Jonathan remains on his back beside Bodhi, blinking up at the ceiling of his home. I'm not sure which giant event proved to be too much for my best friend but suffice to say he's been pushed over his edge.

I take my time standing, holding Seven close. "Are you hurt?"

Seven shakes her head, her eyes lidded. "Are we having a slumber party?"

My heart wants to say yes, to promise her fun times, but I know she needs sleep, or she will be nonfunctional in the morning. "Not tonight. Just a little road trip, is all." My arms are sore, but I manage to step over Bodhi's supine body with Seven scooped in my arms. I am barely keeping up, but I know I won't be able to process anything if I'm in mom-mode. Seven puts up a perfunctory protest about having to go to sleep, but her eyes are already closed, so I don't bother with the debate.

After I tuck her into Jonathan's king-sized bed, I stumble back into the living room, where the guys have managed to sit up, but nothing more than that. My knees tremble as it begins to hit me that my living room exploded, and we are now officially on the run.

Connery whines in my direction, *"I tried to follow ye to help put Seven down, but my legs aren't working yet."*

This magic stuff definitely has some drawbacks.

If there's one thing I've clung to in this whole trial by fire parenting situation, it's that I cannot afford to break down completely. When my sister died, I thought my insides might splinter apart; the grief was so unbearable. But taking in Seven meant that I had to get out of bed every morning. I had to set aside my grief as much as I was able so I could focus on Seven's needs.

Jonathan tells me that's dysfunctional.

I don't know any other way.

While I want to fall apart at the prospect of my home being destroyed, I hold myself together as best I am able. I sit on Jonathan's cream-colored couch, my eyes too wide to close, even though I am exhausted.

Connery lays over my feet to warm them. His front paw drapes over his maw as if he means to hide his face from me.

I reach down to pet him, but that doesn't seem to relax the firm hold he has on his body. "Are you okay, Connery?"

"How can you ask me tha?" comes his inaudible reply. *"Ye just lost your home because of me."*

My insides tighten, but my mind refuses to make room for the trauma. I can only handle so much before I collapse in a pile of anxiety and depression. "I can't think about that right now." My hand remains atop his back. "You didn't do it; those soldiers attacked my home. You don't get to carry the responsibility for their actions. That's for them to answer for. Let's not rob them of their gift of guilt."

Connery turns his head to me, casting up a quizzical look as if I've said something strange. Then he huddles tighter to my legs. *"I will make this up to ye."*

I shake my head at him. "They're not your amends to make. You just focus on getting better, not on taking the blame for something you didn't do."

Despite Bodhi's earlier protest of not deigning to sleep on the floor, he sprawls out on the living room carpet, too depleted to move.

Jonathan's voice is quiet but laced with worry. "Are we safe here, Bodhi?"

The stranger nods, lit only by the lamp on the end table that's set on a timer to be on at night. "Connery will be declared dead because they'll need to save face to the king. If they don't report success on the mission back to the king, they'll all die. Usually by beheading. The soldiers who came after us know Connery is still alive, but they'll never be able to find us, now that my tracker isn't giving off a signal. After a day or so, they'll go back to my world and report a brave conquest over the traitor's dead body."

"What about you?"

"I'm a casualty of war. I'm dead, too. It's easier to lie to the king rather than tell him the job is impossible."

Jonathan frowns. "But those guys saw us disappear. They know we're not dead. Won't they try to track us down still?"

Bodhi shrugs sloppily, his chin lolling to the side. "Maybe for another day or two, but they have no idea where to look." His voice shifts to a sadder note, his arms sprawled on the carpet while he processes all that just happened. "You don't understand what it was like when Connery contracted the disease. He was the king's right hand. Carried out the king's will without a blink because he had no choice in the matter. The bloodiest body count in the land belongs to my best friend. When he got sick with the same thing he was arresting people for having?" Bodhi shakes his head. "There was no one more loyal to the throne than Connery. Everyone had their moments of being surprised when someone they thought was loyal to the throne was taken to the prisons, but Connery being one of them was a shock to us all. Well, it was a shock to everyone who believed the lie the king was spinning, that the disease meant you were disloyal to the throne. People started speaking out, questioning the king about the civilians who were already incarcerated. If Connery was sick, then surely the disease wasn't reserved for the disloyal only."

Jonathan shakes his head. "So much time wasted on a witch hunt. Different world, same sad song. That time and those resources could have been spent finding a cure."

Bodhi chuckles humorlessly. "You know, I think I said the same thing. They don't like to hear that, though. Logic is the enemy of selfish stupidity." Bodhi motions to Connery, who is still clinging to my feet. "Connery was the lightning rod that set everything on its head. People started protesting, talking back. A few of the king's soldiers even laid down their swords, refusing to carry out the king's orders anymore. They knew Connery was unswervingly loyal. They knew they'd been had."

Bodhi's words sizzle in the air for a few beats. Neither Jonathan nor I want to touch them. It's hard to think of a land where the ruler cares more about power than his people.

Then again, maybe it's not so hard to believe after all.

15

FAILED

Jonathan is the grownup tonight since I am too shocked from the loss of my home to put one foot in front of the other without proper prodding.

Jonathan helps me to stand, guiding me by the hand toward the second bedroom in his well-furnished apartment. "We're done with Crimshade economics for the night. You just lost your home. Seven's going to need you coherent in the morning. You know that girl doesn't sleep in on the days you really want her to."

I don't protest, even though I know sleep is going to be a problem for me tonight.

Jonathan leads me to the second bedroom, which is his office with a futon in the corner. I stand in the center of the room while Jonathan sets up his futon. "I'm sleeping in here tonight," he informs me. "Seven's in my bed, which is big enough for the two of you plus one giant dog. I'm taking the futon tonight."

I don't even have the grace to protest us kicking him out of his own bed. I'm too stunned for words.

My condo is in shambles.

Jonathan motions to the small dresser in the closet that is reserved for Seven and me. When it's clear I cannot put the pieces together, he takes pity on me and pulls out a pair of pajamas that I keep at his house. "Go change. Then go to bed." When I don't respond, Jonathan presses the pajamas into my hands, then turns to my dog. "Connery, she needs to sleep. Make sure she gets there? Last door on the left. Quiet, though. Seven needs her sleep, too."

Connery gives him a quiet yip, and then nudges me out the door and toward the bathroom.

I don't want to look at my face in the mirror, so I change with my back to the glass. I don't want to know what I look like when I don't have a home. A cell phone. A couch. A refrigerator.

A plan.

Connery leads me to Jonathan's bedroom once I emerge, leaving Bodhi to help himself to the couch in the living room.

A sliver of moonlight illuminates my baby angel as she sleeps soundly in the center of Jonathan's king-sized bed. She looks so tiny, so innocent.

She's homeless now.

My mother's clock. It's the only thing of my mother's that I kept, and now it's gone.

I'm careful as I climb into the bed, moving Seven to the side so there is room for Connery and me. The moment I slide under the covers, flipping the comforter over the dog by my side, I allow the darkness to see my grief.

Fat tears roll down my cheeks. I know I can't truly fall apart; I have to keep my sadness silent.

But when Connery studies my face up close, his bright blue eyes curiously human as they drink in the scope of my raw emotions, I finally give myself permission to break down.

My lower lip quivers as I whisper my heartbreak to my dog. "They blew up my home."

Connery leans in, pressing his forehead to mine. That one spot of warmth floods me, giving me the courage to feel the hard things I might normally push aside.

"I tried so h-hard to give Seven a good life. Stable. Peaceful." The next words crack out of me with fresh heartbreak. "I f-failed. I've never failed anything before."

Connery licks a few of my tears, sweeping them away even as more replace the ones he erases. He keeps his forehead pressed to mine even as my arms go around him to tug his body closer.

He doesn't burden me with his guilt, though I know he still feels responsible for the altercation. He doesn't make my feelings about him, but lets me have my own, cuddling me close so I can find my way through the muck with a friend.

Just saying the words "I failed" makes them feel truer than I ever thought they could be. It's a gavel falling to declare me unworthy of motherhood—a club I wasn't sure I wanted to join in the first place before my impromptu promotion.

Connery tilts his maw, motioning to Seven, who is sleeping soundly on my other side. *"She's perfect,"* he remarks in that unspoken way.

I roll onto my back, turning my head so I can study the baby I held in my arms minutes after my sister gave birth to her. Back then, I thought she was the most perfect little boy I'd ever seen in my life. Now that she's a girl, my heart *knows* she is the most perfect little girl I've ever seen in my life.

I lost my mother.

I lost my sister.

And now I've lost my home. But as I watch Seven's body move slowly with her breathing, I know that not all is lost.

I bring Connery closer, so his throat rests across my shoulder and his maw is pressed to the side of my face. "Don't leave us?" I whisper, needing my dog to stay with me at least for the night until the world settles to a less harrowing pace.

Connery responds by settling in beside me, his arm draping across my midsection. *"Never."*

All night long, whenever I need to cry all over again, Connery nuzzles my tears until I fall back asleep beside him.

While I can't undo the steps that led me here, Connery is the one part of this that I don't regret in the least.

16

HOME AND HEIST

I sleep in only because when Seven awakes, Connery leads her to the second bedroom for Jonathan to pal around with her. Then Connery rejoins me in the bed, tucking me in and lying beside me so I can go back to sleep.

Since I took Seven in, there have been a limited number of days where I could sleep in. I love the lazy feel of it, the purposeful ignoring of adulthood that's always so insistent I rise to the occasion, no matter the hour. For a whole sixty minutes, I sleep while Jonathan and Seven make breakfast and do their silly morning things that now include Bodhi.

Connery is warm, his head on my shoulder calming me like a weighted blanket. "Let's never leave this bed," I murmur, eyes closed.

"Fine by me."

We lay there snuggled up for several more minutes until guilt taps me on the shoulder. When I finally get out of bed, I am greeted by the sight of Bodhi in a princess crown, sitting at the kitchen table while Jonathan and Seven make breakfast together.

I love Sev in her little pink footie pajamas. There's something so precious and innocent about them that makes me believe she might still be shielded from the worst the world has to offer.

Jonathan is showered and dressed in his khakis and a light blue dress shirt, looking effortlessly put together and pristine, as always. Next to him, I look a mess, but I'm not sure I care just yet. Everything Jonathan does is tasteful and classy, down to the lighting fixture over the table that juts out with black angular mounts for each of the ten bulbs.

This is twice in one week that Jonathan has made me breakfast. I don't know what I would do without him, which is a thought I ponder constantly. "I'm so grateful for you," I tell him as he slides a plate stacked high with pancakes toward me.

It's probably too sincere a thing to say this early, but there's no point in holding back my relief that Jonathan is my best friend.

I need a friend today.

He winks at me. "I'm secretly hoping you'll feel so grateful that you'll make your coconut curry for me."

"Done."

Seven kisses my cheek in between bites of pancakes. "Did we drive here in the middle of the night, Mommy? I was surprised to wake up in Papa Jonathan's house. I was like, 'How did I get here?'" Her eyes bug to demonstrate her surprise.

Even though I was hungry just a second ago, my stomach rejects the idea of food now. My mouth turns to sand while I gear up to deliver the grave news. "Honey, something bad happened last night, so we had to leave." I'm glad I let Connery outside, so he doesn't have to relive this. However, I can feel Bodhi's eyes on me from behind. I'm guessing he's standing in the entryway to the kitchen, listening to how this is going to be retold. "Some soldiers from Crimshade showed up while you were sleeping. They wanted to take Connery and Bodhi away just because they're sick with those booboos we saw on them. Instead of focusing on treating their illness, those soldiers wanted to throw Connery and Bodhi into prison for the crime of getting sick."

Seven gasps, her little face aghast that the world could be so cruel.

Girl, I feel you.

"No!" Her eyes alight on Bodhi over my shoulder. "We won't let them take you!"

I nod, swallowing hard. "We escaped here, but the soldiers destroyed our home." My heart is heavy as I deliver the bad news. "We can't go back there."

Jonathan clears his throat. "My friend of a friend who

works at the police station informed me this morning that the two of you are being declared dead. Might be a good thing, given the circumstances."

My stomach drops at the news I didn't see coming. "What?"

Seven squeaks as she tries to keep up. Her little hand flies over her mouth. "We're dead? Like Mommy?"

It's the punch in the gut I didn't see coming. I can't even focus on my own shock; so ripe is Seven's grief. "They only *think* we're dead, baby. Thanks to Bodhi, you and I are just fine. Not a scratch."

Seven's lips purse as she processes a very big concept. "But we're not dead. We can just tell them they made a mistake."

I shake my head, though I wish it was that simple. "Right now, we need to help Bodhi and Connery, which is harder to do if those soldiers keep coming after us. It will help them stay safer if those bad guys think we're all dead."

Seven lowers her head, her dark waves falling forward. She takes a minute to gather her courage, her thoughts, and her broken heart. When she lifts her chin, it's with a determination that she will somehow make this work. "My toys are gone?"

Why is it always me who has to deliver the hard truths? Being a parent is rough.

I nod, crossing my arms over my chest to bolster my

matter-of-factness, which is what she needs from me in this moment. "Yep."

"My pink fuzzy reading chair?"

"Gone."

"The pictures of Mommy?"

I hold up my hand. "Those are all backed up in the cloud. Those stay with us forever. They're safe."

Seven nods, though she doesn't look relieved. "I'm not going to school if I'm dead, right?"

"Nope. Homeschool for you, babe."

She sits straighter in her chair. "Okay." She spears her pancakes nonchalantly, as if nothing traumatizing just happened.

"Really? It's that simple?" I know I shouldn't question it. I'm sure the devastation will pop up in time for her. But I want the other shoe to drop now, while I'm ready for it.

Seven shrugs. "I don't have to go to school. I'm good. I mean, eventually I'm going to want more toys, but for now I'll take it. Nathan calls me a boy still. When Olivia's mad, she tells me I can't use the girls' bathroom. And the substitute teachers always call me the wrong name. I don't want to go back there."

It's my turn to be the baby, to let emotions take me over when Seven is determined to process the perks like an adult. I forsake my seat and rush to her, scooping my little angel in my arms in the most dramatic of fashions. "I'm so sorry this happened," I whisper. "And I'm sorry those children haven't been raised to be kind. That's not on you;

that's on them." I squeeze her tighter. "I know who you are. I know you're a girl. Never stop telling me who you are because I'll always want to know you."

Seven squeezes me around the neck, her cheek pressed to mine. "I will. Right now, I'm glad I don't have to go back there."

"You never have to see those kids again."

Seven nods. "I'm going to want some toys, though," she reminds me. "Do we live with Papa Jonathan now? And Bodhi is my brother?"

I can't bring myself to make eye contact with Jonathan, silently asking him if we can stay. My pride can't take the hit of asking for this much help.

Jonathan holds up his hand. "I have two rules before I decide if you can stay with me forever." His serious face makes my stomach hollow. "Rule number one: Papa Jonathan demands a hug as often as you need one. I mean it, Sev. If you need a hug and you don't take one from me, I'm going to get real cross. I might even send you to bed with only one dessert."

Seven cracks a smile. "Deal!" She squirms to get down and runs to him. "I need a hug! Emergency!"

Jonathan scoops her up while she squeezes him around the neck. "Don't get comfortable. Rule number two is a rough one." He holds up two fingers for Seven and me to see. "Rule number two: I still want to be the dad."

Seven peppers his face with kisses. "Deal! I love you, Papa Jonathan!"

Jonathan giggles through his faux stern face. "Don't get too excited. Being your dad means I get to use my dad voice. I can say things like, 'It's time for bed,' and 'Eat your vegetables.'"

She hugs him around the neck until his eyes bug. "You're my favorite dad of all the dads in all the worlds."

When Seven beams at me from Jonathan's arms with a cheery, "Mommy, you haven't touched your pancakes," my heart melts. The worries I harbored mere seconds ago begin to fall to the wayside as I slink to my seat.

But I hate it. I hate receiving help, especially as big as this. Doing the helping makes me come alive. Taking the help feels like a gut punch to my pride from which I worry I might never recover.

Bodhi comes further into the kitchen, taking the third seat while Jonathan slides a stack of pancakes in front of him. He stares at the fluffy breakfast, but instead of digging in, he stares up at us with a wistful melancholy. "You're good people. Like, really good." He manages a semblance of a smile. "Enjoy every minute of having such a generous family, lovely Petunia."

Seven munches on her breakfast after Jonathan sets her back in her seat. "Zara's your mom too, you know. And Jonathan can be your dad." She tilts her head to the side. "Do you have good parents? Or is your first mom dead, like mine?"

It's her trauma to talk about but hearing her say "dead" so casually knocks the wind out of me.

Bodhi picks up his fork, eating like a proper gentleman. "My upbringing wasn't like yours. Whether my parents died or gave me up, I was never told."

Horror washes over Seven's face. She rushes to his side, throwing her arms around him. "They're fools, all of them! I'm so sorry, Bodhi. We want you! We think you're the best boy that ever was."

Bodhi chuckles at her affection, but I can tell he loves it. Perhaps he even needs it.

Bodhi ruffles Seven's hair and then sends her back to her seat. "It all worked out. I'm perfectly fine. I had three brothers growing up. Not blood brothers, mind you, but Connery, Fritz, and Felix? They're the only family I've ever known," he pauses to wink at her, "until now."

Seven's mouth screw to the side. "How did your world get invented?"

It's a left field question, but one I probably should have thought to ask.

Bodhi straightens his suspender thoughtfully. "Well, a very long time ago, a god named Dub created Crimshade in an explosion of glimmering black light. It was beautiful back then when the world was new. Tall, Crimshade trees stretching to the sky. Green grass. Utopia. But then Dub left us, and without someone to keep the world spinning, men became greedy and nature grew unruly. Now there are no Crimshade trees left, and the rulers we've had are afraid of no one, knowing that Dub will do nothing, and the Goddess of Vengeance has deserted the land."

Seven scratches her nose. "The Goddess of Vengeance?"

Bodhi nods. "Indeed. Lore states that the Goddess of Vengeance will come to Crimshade and set right all the wrongs that have been inflicted upon the people in Dub's absence."

"Where is Dub? Did he die?" Seven asks as I let Connery back inside.

"He's immortal, so no, he didn't die." Bodhi shrugs with a tightness to his shoulders. "He simply doesn't care about us anymore."

Jonathan sits in the fourth seat at the table after setting a plate of pancakes on the floor for Connery. "Okay, enough history lessons. We need a plan. I can go out and buy more clothes and toiletries and whatnot for you all, but I think the real issue is what to do about your identities. Telling the police you somehow survived the explosion will only lead the Crimshade villains straight to you. For now, you stay inside and let the police believe what they believe." Jonathan shoots me a look filled with meaning, and I know what he's thinking as he speaks. "Maybe we let them believe you're dead forever."

He's thinking, as I am, that perhaps it would be safer for Seven if she and I stayed dead and created new lives for ourselves. One where she can be a girl to a new group of peers so that someone this young doesn't have to deal with such harsh ostracization.

It's not the road I want to travel, but if we don't want

the Crimshade soldiers coming for us, it might be the only path forward.

I nod, chewing slowly. "Then we're starting over."

Though, I have no idea how one does that. Start over? Where will we live while I get a new job and save up for a place? How will I take care of her with no money?

My elbows rest on the table so I can grind my knuckles into my temples, searching for a better solution.

Jonathan is part magic, I am certain, because he reads my mind as if I've spoken aloud. "You'll stay here with me."

I lower my head, accepting his help because I literally have no other options. It's a hit to my pride, but I've learned you cannot have both a child and pride. "Thank you. We'll stay with you until I can save up for a new place."

Jonathan's jaw tightens. "That's nothing you'll ever have to worry about. You can stay with me forever. I've got your back, Zara. You know that. Let me do this."

I shake my head, staring at him without bothering to conceal the sadness radiating from my soul. "I have nothing. No money. No job. Give me a couple of months, and I'll get us squared away in a new place."

Jonathan pretends to pout. "Only a couple of months? Come on, Zara. Don't cut the slumber party short on my account." He motions to Seven, who couldn't be cheerier that we get to stay with Jonathan. "You two are my only chance to have a family. Let me do this. Let me be happy."

Sure, being gay presents a person with a different set of hurdles when it comes to getting married and having children. But Jonathan's bigger issue stems from the fact that he is allergic to long-term romantic relationships.

I know because we are the same in that way.

I close my eyes, horrified and humiliated that all my hard work has crumbled, leading me to this dire moment. I don't have the words to agree or argue, so I merely bob my head.

I love him.

But I hate this.

I lower my head in defeat. "Thank you, Jonathan."

Bodhi chuckles at me. "Wow. That looked painful."

"It was," I admit.

Jonathan cracks his knuckles against his cheek. "Good. Now that that's out of the way, let's figure out a heist."

Seven's head tilts to the side. "What's a heist?"

Jonathan feathers his fingers together. "Remember Robin Hood? Steals from the rich to feed the poor? Well, we're going to figure out a way to get as many bottles of antibiotics as possible so we can take them to the prisoners in Crimshade. Then Bodhi and Connery can return home heroes."

Bodhi snorts, as if nothing could be further from the outcome we are walking into. "The only thing the king hates worse than disloyal subjects is a hero. We'll go about the business of curing the prisoners quietly. Once we have enough of us back on our feet, we can petition to be set free."

I run my hand over my face as the long road ahead seems to stretch out endlessly.

But it's the right thing to do—helping these people who don't have access to the right medicine.

I eat my pancakes while Connery coils his tail around my ankle, tethering me to the conversation when the weight of it all threatens to be too much to handle.

17

ROBIN HOOD

"This was a bad idea," I tell Jonathan. "Bodhi's going in there, but he doesn't know what he's looking for. It's all locked up too, so even if he gets in undetected, how's he going to get what we need?"

Letting Jonathan pick my clothes means that I am far more colorful and fashionable than ever before. However, I fail to see how a snug red V-neck sweater and black skinny jeans are going to make me more incognito when my curves stand out from a mile away, even under cover of the moonlit darkness.

Bodhi leans forward in the backseat of my green sedan. "We thought of everything. Connery is with Seven back home, so she's secured. Jonathan went back to your home and took your car, so we have a getaway vehicle that isn't Jonathan's, so as not to incriminate him. Plus, Seven loaned me a book and crayons back here, so I'm covered as far as entertainment goes."

I roll my eyes at him and sink down in the driver's seat, the brim of my black baseball hat tilted over my face as much as possible. "We're going to get caught. We're going to go to jail!"

Jonathan rests his hand atop my wrist. "We're parking in the lot just there, not at the pharmacy. Bodhi's going to walk over and break in. He'll steal everything he needs and be back out, no problem."

Bodhi ticks off the points we went over in his flash-flood induction into modern security systems. "I'll need to pass through the door without opening it, so I don't trigger the alarm. That's not a problem." He grimaces. "Well, it's not a problem if I can do it without fainting. Passing through a solid door requires far more magic than merely unlocking it without a key."

Jonathan's brows pinch. "I really need you to not faint inside the pharmacy. We can't go in there and get you out without alerting the police of what we're doing."

Bodhi leans back in his seat. "So, if I faint..."

"You can't faint," Jonathan insists. "The whole plan thrives on anonymity."

"When I faint," Bodhi continues, "the best way to revive me is splashing water on my face. I assume you people don't have lavender tonic."

"You assume right." Jonathan grabs up a bottle of

water he keeps in his car. "But again, we can't go in there and help you. If you faint, you're on your own."

"Glad to hear it. Well, the mission might take longer, then."

I pinch the bridge of my nose. "Look, I left a dog in charge of my daughter. We're going in and out, and that's that. Is it harder for you to pass two people through the door?"

Bodhi perks up. "I thought you'd never ask. Body mass is a factor, so you'd be better to take than Jonathan."

I tug the brim of my black baseball cap lower over my forehead. "Let's do this." I snatch up the bottle of water and exit the car as soon as we park.

My best friend shoots me a look of warning, as if I don't know how bad the consequences will be if we're caught.

My heart pounds as my feet carry me through two parking lots toward the pharmacy. There are several in town, but this is the largest one.

I don't know how many antibiotics we'll find inside. I can only hope it's enough that we don't have to do this again.

Bodhi scoops up my hand, giving me the second duffle bag to loop over my shoulder. "Slower," he cautions me. "We don't want to draw attention to ourselves. We're just two people out for a late-night stroll."

I take his advice, but it doesn't calm my pulse in the

least. I can't remember the last time I held a man's hand who wasn't Jonathan.

"This will really cure my people?" Bodhi asks, revealing a raw nerve.

My head bobs. "Two weeks of antibiotics should do the trick. So, we'll want one bottle per person. How many do you guess are infected?"

Bodhi's voice turns grave. "The prison was so full; they had more bodies than cells. Thousands, Zara."

My jaw tightens. I kinda wish I hadn't asked. "Then we've got our work cut out for us."

When we reach the back entrance of the pharmacy, I turn my chin expectantly up at Bodhi. "How does this work?"

I probably should have asked that before we left the car.

"Very carefully, is how. Hold tight to my hand."

We both squeeze the other's fingers in the night as Bodhi begins a series of deep breaths. I wonder if I should be helping in some way. In the movies, magical creatures can simply pass through walls all willy-nilly, without wear and tear to their energy. But this seems more akin to gearing up to run a long race.

"Close your eyes and go where I lead you."

On instinct, I don't want to do any part of that. I don't know Bodhi well enough to trust him to lead me anywhere, and I don't want to close my eyes while that's happening.

Still, this is part of the job, so I do as he requests, even though it goes against my stubborn nature. The sooner this is done, the sooner I can get back to Seven and Connery.

My nerves spike as Bodhi brings me in front of him to face the door, leaning me forward so our bodies are pressed against the hard surface. His chin loops over my shoulder as we inhale the chilled air together. A few more deep breaths, and he slides his body behind mine, pinning me to the door in a manner that is somehow unthreatening.

"Three breaths together, then we fall through. If I faint..."

"I splash water on your face."

I can hear the smirk in his voice. "If you were Jonathan, I would make a crack about you kissing me back to life."

I chuckle, my ribs moving against his. "Jonathan would never fall for that."

We take three deliberate breaths together before we lean into the door. The hard surface presents the expected resistance, but then begins to soften, like it's being melted while still holding its shape. My brows raise even as I keep my eyes closed. "It's working!"

"Surprised? I should think you'd be impressed. I settle for nothing less than absolute fireworks."

"I dare you to say that to Jonathan before you kiss him."

"Deal." Bodhi presses my body with more force, and slowly, the two of us move through the malleable surface as if wading through very stiff Jell-O.

I stumble forward, my chest heaving because we actually did it.

Bodhi's weight on my back is heavier than I anticipated. When he faints, as he warned me he would, we both hit the ground on our knees.

My palms smart, but after I collect my bearings, I make quick work of rolling him off me, so his back is lain on the floor. Then I unscrew the cap on the bottle so I can flick water on his face.

Bodhi's angular features are lit only by the red glow from the exit sign.

Over and over, I flick water at him, but he doesn't stir. Panicking, I shake his shoulders, but that also proves useless.

Breathless and scared, I lean down, whispering in his ear a tense, "I'll get the antibiotics; you have until I get back to wake up or I will soundly kick your hairy butt."

I am positive the threat is useless.

I stand with all discernable caution, keeping my hat tugged over my face as I move toward the rows and rows of pills. I know offhand a few names of the antibiotics and steroids I've taken over the years, but Jonathan printed out a comprehensive list that I swiped from Bodhi's pocket.

I really need a flashlight.

If there was ever confirmation that a life of crime is not for me, it is how ill-prepared I am for this heist.

I make my way through the aisles, gathering up anything and everything I can find that might prove useful, and shove it in the duffle over my shoulder.

The bottles clack together, the pills making music with every step I take. I pull packs, boxes, and bottles from the shelves, then I pass something I know Jonathan takes that costs him a pretty penny. It's not easy to live with HIV, especially when the medicine to keep the disease at bay is ridiculously (and often prohibitively) expensive.

I scoop the lot of it into the duffel, grateful that I can pay Jonathan back in some way for taking us in.

I search for more antibiotics and steroids, making sure I'm exhausting the printout for each name listed, so I don't skip over anything that might prove useful. My gaze snags on multivitamins, which I didn't realize you could get a prescription for, so I add those to the duffle as well. I'm guessing prisoners aren't terribly well-nourished and could probably use a vitamin boost.

Once the duffle is full, I tiptoe to Bodhi, sliding his bag from his side so I can fill that as well.

We selected the largest pharmacy in the area. I hope they have enough antibiotics on hand, so we don't have to do this all over again.

Vitamins for myself, Jonathan and Seven go into the bag, along with antiseptic, lotions and extra strength pain killers, just in case.

It's not until my eyes flit across something I've known our family will need in the future that I pause, my heart thudding afresh.

There it is. If Seven had been born female and went into puberty to early, this is the medicine that would stop that process so she didn't start her period at like, age seven or something far too young. It's perfectly safe and has been used for years on children to keep early puberty from settling in until the child is old enough to handle it. It's apparently being prescribed here without issue to little girls who need that assistance.

It's the same medicine that transgender children use to stop puberty from setting in when that would further exacerbate their unrest. It would stop Seven's voice from dropping when she hits that age. It doesn't do anything long-term, and it's completely reversible if needed. But legislators don't bother to consult with doctors, most of whom understand that this is a lifesaving medicine for transgender children, who suffer from a disproportionately higher risk of suicide.

This is something we won't be able to get for her in my state.

I take the entire box of the stuff, throwing my middle finger in the air at all the government officials who would rather see my child dead than comfortable in her own body.

Some people might say that's an extreme conclusion.

I say it's not their kid they'll have to bury if I'm right.

Anger wells in the shreds of my soul, but I stuff it down and thank fate for letting my baby have the medicine she needs—even if I have to steal it.

I gasp when I find a freshly stocked stash of antibiotics in a cabinet. My arm moves along the shelves to quickly sweep the contents into the second duffle.

I don't like the idea of stealing, but there is no conceivable way to heal these magical people without this medication. And I can't exactly liberate them all from prison to bring them here for a physical.

There are so many variants of the antibiotics on the list, and they're not all in one spot, so it takes me precious time to troll the shelves until I get to the bottom of my long list, and the top of both duffels.

When every inch is packed and the bags barely zip shut, I make my way back to Bodhi's side. I drop to my knees, guessing that he should be awake by now.

"The water was supposed to work!" I whisper, trying not to freak out and failing miserably as my pulse spikes. My heart pounds from the criminal activity, and the very real possibility that we might not get away with it.

Sweat dots my upper lip as I unscrew the cap and dump the entire bottle of water on Bodhi's face. It gets up his nose and trickles into his parted lips. I've never waterboarded anyone before, and I can't believe that's what I'm doing now.

I also can't believe it works.

Bodhi coughs, spluttering and choking, his eyes bugged as his hands flail.

I nearly weep with relief. I turn him onto his side so he can cough up the rest of the water in his lungs. "I'm sorry!" I whisper. "Are you okay?"

Bodhi manages to sit up with my help. "Did you get the stuff?"

I nod, tapping the duffels. "We need to get out of here. Are you up for it?"

"Of course, love. I settle for nothing less than absolute fireworks, remember?" Bodhi's lidded, wry expression does not instill much hope in me, nor does his clumsy attempt to stand. He leans heavily on me, reaching out toward the door and missing.

"You're scaring me," I admit in a terse hiss. "Please tell me you can get us out of here!"

Bodhi responds by smooshing my body between his and the door, just like we did on our way in. I hold tight to both duffels, scared and grateful that this might actually work. "Drag my body to the car, will you? Don't ditch me in your world."

I reach behind me and grab onto his hand, my check pressed to the cold door. "Never. You'll return to Crimshade a hero."

Bodhi chuckles. "Oh, that sweet optimism. I'll miss it when we part ways."

I guess that never occurred to me. But of course we'll go our separate ways when this is all over. There's no need for me to cross into his world. It would be irresponsible to take Seven to a land riddled with corruption.

I should keep my mouth shut instead of speaking my fears aloud. Bodhi needs to concentrate on getting us out of here, after all. But insecurity overrides my need for logic to be the clear winner. "Connery isn't staying with us, is he."

Bodhi shakes his head, crushing my body to the door with his weight. "I'm afraid not. He'll return with me so he can clear his name and set things right. A fair amount of people are in jail because he put them there on the king's orders. He'll want to be part of the liberation. His soul needs the redemption."

My heart sinks as despair chokes me around the throat. "Oh. That makes sense." But the thought of losing my dog riddles me with a weight that I cannot shake.

How I've loved sleeping beside Connery every night. It's going to break Seven's little heart when we have to let him go.

Not to mention the state of my own torn apart heart.

The only thing that snaps me out of my impending bought of depression is when the door turns to Jell-O, and Bodhi's body pushes me through it.

This time, I can feel his tension, as if it is taking up far more of his energy and effort to get us through the solid surface. Who knew magic was so arduous? In the movies, it's a twitch of a nose, a flick of a wand. But Bodhi cries out in actual pain as we sink through and come out the other side, bathed in moonlight.

Sure enough, Bodhi passes clean out atop me. I take a steadying breath after I extract myself from his body and manage to stand, but my knees are shaking.

I pretend it's from the blast of icy air.

It takes me longer than I would like, exposed to the night as I am, to gather the gumption needed to drag Bodhi to safety. The pill bottles clack loudly in the duffels, banging at my sides. I feel horrible that Bodhi's back is dragging over uneven chunks of pavement and parking lot debris. But not even the discomfort is enough to rouse him from his slumber of utter depletion.

Magic sure is a lot of work.

Jonathan could drive to meet us, but then my car and license plate would get picked up by the outside cameras. It's a long way to the car three lots over, but I know I don't have the option of giving up. I drag a full-grown man step by step, trying not to grunt so I don't draw attention to myself from anyone driving by. I look like I'm dragging a dead body, which I truly hope is not the case.

When I finally get to the car, I shove the duffels in the trunk and do my best to hoist Bodhi up under his armpits, hefting his top half into the backseat. I managed to lift Connery several times, but Bodhi is taller, and I wasn't carrying bulky bags filled with medicine when I hoisted up my dog.

"Stay where you are," I remind Jonathan. "You're not wearing a hat or anything to hide your face. I've got this."

I really don't got this. It takes an embarrassingly long time to negotiate Bodhi's long body into the backseat of the car, and even then, I nearly shut the door on his leg because it keeps flopping out like limp spaghetti.

I keel over when I shove myself into the passenger's seat, motioning for Jonathan to drive.

My best friend's eyes are wide as he starts up the engine. "Are you okay? Did you get the antibiotics and steroids?"

"All they had," I confirm, exhausted and absolutely done with this night. "Home. Shower. Bed."

Jonathan turns onto the main road. "You got it."

Though we are safe and on our way home, my heart won't stop pounding.

I just committed a crime in the dark of night—not against a person who wronged my daughter, but against a whole institution. I can only hope my illegal deeds stay hidden from the daylight, otherwise an entire prison filled with innocent people will wither and rot with no hope of help.

18

HUGS AND WATERBOARDING

Am I worried that Bodhi still hasn't stirred, even after Jonathan does a fireman's carry to bring our incapacitated friend into the house?

No, I'm petrified.

The goal wasn't to sacrifice one of Crimshade's citizens to heal the sick. The goal was to help everyone.

I can't even enjoy the sight of Connery with a pillowcase affixed to his head like a bride's veil; so acute is my worry.

Seven's little hands ball into fists beside her cheeks—a thing she does when she's freaking out. "Bodhi! Bodhi, wake up!"

So much for Connery making sure Seven went to sleep at a reasonable hour. It's nearing eleven o'clock at night.

I run to the bathroom, motioning for Jonathan to follow me with his cargo. I turn on the warm water in the tub, hoping there is some Heavenly pardon for people who have to waterboard someone to help them.

Twice in one night.

While stealing medicine from a pharmacy.

I grimace as I realize that my conscience has taken a huge hit tonight.

Jonathan lowers Bodhi to the gold-colored bathmat with a grunt, then stretches out his back. "If anyone asks, I carried a grown man with no sweat whatsoever. I'm just that strong."

I salute his lie and then drop to my knees, removing Bodhi's shoes and socks. He's always so dapper; I guess he might not be too excited if his things are soaked through. I remove his suspenders, but that's all I'm willing to do. The rest is just going to have to get wet. Most of him already is from being dragged across the slushy ground.

"Got one more 'oomph' in you? We need to get Bodhi inside the tub. Water was the only thing that worked on him before."

Jonathan cracks his neck. "I've got one embarrassingly dramatic 'oomph'. Prepare thyself."

I don't know how Jonathan keeps his humor in situations like these, but I'm grateful for the over-the-top noises he makes trying to get Bodhi into the tub. The two of us do our best not to knock the lanky man's head or arms on anything that might inflict a bruise by morning.

My chest heaves as I motion toward the door. "Get me a cup."

Jonathan ambles to the kitchen and comes back with Seven on his heels. "Out you go, munchkin. You may have conned Connery out of going to bed, but I'm your dad, so I get to say things like, 'Only one dessert after dinner,' and 'Go to bed if you want to find a truckload of presents under the Christmas tree this year.'"

Seven claps her hands and squeals. "Can I have a new doll? A transgender one with brown skin who looks like me?"

"You can have a freaking pony if you go to bed right now without a bedtime story."

She hops, taking his wish as a directive. "Okay, Papa Jonathan! I love you, Bodhi! Have a good bubble bath! Oo! A dog and a pony in the same year? Best dad ever!" Then she runs to put herself to bed, which I know has a short shelf life. The girl needs a bedtime story and the bedtime song. She'll be back once she realizes she's been shorted.

"You realize you now have to buy her either a doll that doesn't exist or an actual pony, right?"

Jonathan winces. "I just put that together. I'll figure it out. First things first: why isn't Bodhi waking up?"

"You might want to leave the room for this."

Jonathan's brows furrow. "Why?"

Sweat beads on my forehead. "Because I have to waterboard him, and I don't want you to know I'm capable of doing something so horrible!"

Connery is in the doorway, his makeshift veil gone as

he watches the situation with a discerning eye. *"Do it,"* he rules in his nonverbal manner. *"It's the only way."*

Jonathan doesn't leave but stays by my side while I fill the cup under the cold spray and then pour a steady stream over Bodhi's nose and mouth.

I hate that I've seen enough crime dramas that I know how to do this. Somewhere my mother is shaking her finger at me, reminding me how many times she told me those shows would rot my brain.

Or corrupt me completely.

Bodhi doesn't stir. Panic strikes me as I refill the cup and pour a steadier stream over his nose and mouth, hoping for forgiveness, and for Bodhi to open his eyes.

On second thought, I'll trade the forgiveness in exchange for Bodhi opening his eyes.

I nearly cry when Bodhi chokes.

Jonathan yanks his torso out of the tub to Heimlich Bodhi over the ledge to get the water out of his nose, mouth, and probably lungs.

Bodhi's eyes are wide as he coughs and splutters, holding onto Jonathan's forearms as he fights to steady himself through the shock to his system.

In a move that is one hundred percent my best friend, Jonathan angles Bodhi's torso upward so he can drape Bodhi's arms around his neck. He hugs the woozy man, propping him upright so that the first thing our guest is greeted with after the discomfort wears off is kindness.

I don't expect for Bodhi to sag in Jonathan's embrace

long after he stops coughing, nor for his eyes to close as if this is the affection he's been deprived of for far too long.

I don't imagine many people working in brothels are treated to hugs with no agenda.

Jonathan closes his eyes as well, his hand moving to cup the back of Bodhi's head. "It's going to be okay," he assures the man quietly.

"No," Bodhi protests in a whisper. I can hear his heartbreak plain in the air, his voice thick with unbridled emotion. "It's going to be impossible. It's going to break us all. It's never going to be okay. It's only going to be long and difficult, until I cease to be."

Jonathan clutches Bodhi tighter. He doesn't brush away Bodhi's feelings but holds the man while Bodhi's heart is too heavy to carry on his own. "I know it seems that way. But you're not alone in this anymore."

Jonathan said those exact words to me when my sister passed and I had a breakdown over knowing nothing about how to raise a child that the law and fate handed to me. It was one of the few times I let Jonathan hug me, which was how I started crying in the first place.

Lesson learned. If I want to hold myself together, I can't let someone near enough to hug me.

Jonathan's voice is gentle. "It's not all on your shoulders to redeem your people and set them free so they can stand against a corrupt government."

"It's not enough. All I'm trying to accomplish? It's never enough."

Jonathan's fingers tangle in Bodhi's wet, chaotic hair. "Have you seen this one when she takes on a project?" He jerks his head toward me. "All we have to do is buckle up and pray for daylight. Zara doesn't back down from a challenge. She's a firm believer that the bad guy dies in the end." Jonathan presses his cheek to Bodhi's. "She settles for nothing less than absolute fireworks."

Bodhi snorts into Jonathan's shoulder at his own words echoing in the bathroom.

I manage a small smile of appreciation for Jonathan's magnanimous compliment. But in truth, I have no idea what step two will need to be. We barely made it through step one alive.

I leave Jonathan and Bodhi to the bathroom and stumble out into the hallway. I make it three steps before I slump to the floor, my adrenaline crashing almost violently as my back slides down the wall. I pull my knees to my chest while tears birth and fall down my cheeks.

Damn it. I caught emotions just by being near a hug.

Having a dog is the best blessing I could have asked for. Connery isn't designed to let me cry alone. He moves to my side, licking my cheek until I turn my head to face him. I'm sure I look a mess—puffy eyes and red nose—but Connery doesn't care about any of that. He only cares that I'm sad. He wants to make it better.

Oh, how I've needed a dog exactly like this one in my life.

"Bodhi will be alright," Connery assures me.

"*I'm* not alright!" I whisper. "I waterboarded a man twice in one night. You know who does that? Bond villains! Bad guys! I know I was doing it to help, but I still did it! I didn't know I was capable of something so awful. And I stole, Connery! I stole medicine. Again, I know it's for the greater good, but I don't want to be a person who steals!"

Connery doesn't know how to talk me out of my existential crisis, so he simply rests his head on my shoulder, knowing that when I pet him, my anxiety declines. "*Wherever ye are, there will I be,*" he promises.

I open my mouth to tell him thank you, but I hear Seven's voice down the hall in Jonathan's bedroom. "Mommy? I didn't get a bedtime story or the song. Can you put me to bed?"

And just like that, I'm back on the clock. I don my cheery voice I can always locate if it's for my sweet babe. "Absolutely. Be there in a minute, honey."

I dry my face on the hem of my red shirt and kiss the top of Connery's massive head before I stand.

That was enough time for feelings anyway.

19

POTIONS AND PROTEIN SHAKE

onnery has watched me like a hawk since my breakdown last night. Neither of us knows what to do with me when I go over the edge like that, which is why I rarely tiptoe near the ocean of emotions I don't want to feel.

Bodhi doesn't join us for breakfast. In fact, it's not until noon that he stirs from the guest futon that Jonathan helped him to last night. He's wearing Jonathan's pajamas, which are baggy on his lanky frame. Most troubling are the purple hollows of his eyes, which make him look as if he has been malnourished and deprived of sleep for weeks.

Compassion wells in me as I offer my shoulder for Bodhi to lean on. It's an effort for him just to make it to the table, where Seven is assembling her potions.

Thank goodness Jonathan doesn't mind a mess. Seven

likes to take water, vegetable oil, food coloring and glitter, and mix them all in various containers. Then she labels them as being the perfect antidote for different maladies.

It's cute when it's at my house, but I worry that Jonathan will regret having us over when all his containers are filled with sparkly liquid, and he realizes he is doomed to battle remnants of glitter all over his house for all eternity.

I assemble Bodhi a sandwich while Seven prattles on about which potion would be most helpful if he needs an energy boost.

To his credit, Bodhi plays along to the best of his ability, but eventually veers off into actual mage knowledge. "If you want a true strength tonic, you'll need toad spawn, preferably found under the light of a full moon. Of course, that depends a great deal on just how strong you want to be. If you want to merely be stronger, any old toad spawn will do. But if you want to amaze even your worst enemies, then you'll need to find it under the glow of a full moon in springtime. It's the only way to really put your opponent to shame."

Seven mashes her lips together, and I can tell she is fighting the urge to go out right now and find toad spawn. But she remains at the table, as it is not a full moon, nor is it even nighttime, and the light dusting of snow outside assures her that springtime is nowhere near.

I assemble my own potion in a blender, throwing

together the ingredients for a basic protein smoothie, guessing that might help Bodhi recover a little quicker.

I sit down beside him at the table and slide the glass over. "Drink."

Bodhi sniffs it and recoils. "What is it?"

I roll my eyes. "Poison."

Bodhi leans toward the glass, peering inside. "Smells like it."

"Just drink it." I point to the pills he needs to take to stay on his antibiotics and dose of steroids. "Take that, too. Then you'll be double poisoned."

Seven adds an evil witch cackle just for effect.

Gotta love her.

I sit back in my seat with Connery's head across my thigh. "We need to map out a plan of what to do next. How do we get you to your homeland with the duffel bags? Is there a portal? A ritual? A chant?"

Bodhi takes a sip of the smoothie and grimaces. "Oh, that's dreadful."

I wait for him to give me the barest bit of information so we can make a plan together. I don't want Jonathan to come home from work and find that I've only cleaned his house, made dinner, and done nothing to move the job along. I really don't want our nefarious activities to have been for nothing.

Bodhi takes a bite of his sandwich while he ponders what our next step should be. "There's a way to get from your world to ours, yes. But they'll be monitoring blips of magic, which they will most definitely feel when I go back there. I don't have the foggiest of how I'm going to cross over without alerting the king's mage. He'll will send out every soldier who currently thinks I'm dead if he catches wind of me returning."

I frown. "But surely you're not the only mage. How will the king's dude be sure it's you coming back into Crimshade?"

Bodhi closes his eyes with his long inhale. "My magic is not like the others. I don't know if you noticed last night, but it's weak. Barely worth calling myself a mage, to be honest. My magic feels different to someone like Highbron (that's the king's mage). Not many have a weak blip like mine. And frankly, most of the mages have been locked away in prison."

I purse my lips, trying not to poke at Bodhi's obvious wound. "Invisibility potion? Is that a thing?"

Seven hops up and grabs one of her glittery concoctions, bringing it over to Bodhi with victory certain on her tiny features. "I made one!"

Bodhi always strikes me as too superior to bother with playtime, but he smiles at Seven, taking the container and studying it in the light. "Interesting mix here. I think it needs a week to cure. What do you guess? We want it at its full potency. It won't do if only my left elbow turns invisible."

Seven's shoulders slump. "Rats, I thought I cracked it." Then she returns to her potion making, singing a song about rats that absolutely drives me bonkers, but I pretend to love it.

Bodhi pinches the bridge of his nose. "The pills we stole last night. How many bottles are there? How many prisoners can we cure?"

"Six-hundred-thirteen," I reply, having counted them when I woke up with Jonathan to make him coffee and a disgusting protein shake before he left for work this morning.

Bodhi shakes his head. "I hate to say that it's not enough, because neither of us wants that to be the case, but it's nowhere near enough. We have to pull another heist. Maybe three more."

I lean my head back, groaning aloud. "You barely made it through the first one, Bodhi. We need a better plan."

Bodhi stares at his drink as if he is avoiding looking directly at me. "I could try a vonding charm."

At this, Connery growls. I can tell he does not like that idea one bit. He coils his tail around my leg protectively, making it clear that this charm, whatever it is, will not involve me.

"What's that?" I ask.

"It would tie me to a person just long enough that I could borrow some of their fortitude to get the job done. Then I wouldn't be so depleted."

"Tell me the risks. How would it affect me?"

Connery's head snaps in my direction. "*No,*" I hear

him say.

Bodhi leans back in his seat, reaching for more academic language, as if the whole thing is theoretical, rather than actually happening. "Well, the practice is a tad controversial because mages aren't meant to share their magic, which is essentially what this is, only in reverse. In this case, the mage would be borrowing some of the lifeforce of non-mage. It's a short-term transaction, in which the mage's magic increases while the two are linked. Then when the link fades, the mage's magic goes back to normal, and the lender returns to their normal strength. Vonding is a mix of the words, 'vitality' and 'bonding'."

"But how would it affect me? Would it make me sleepy? Would I have to be the one getting waterboarded to wake me up?" The thought is upsetting on many levels, but that doesn't deter me.

Bodhi angles his body to mine. "Honestly, I don't know. It's old magic. I've never known anyone who's done this. My knowledge is purely academic and not rooted in real life experience."

Seven is playing with her potions, so I'm not sure she's entirely paying attention to our conversation, thank goodness.

"What sorts of supplies do you need to make the spell happen?"

Bodhi shrugs. "It's a chant, a red cord around our wrists, and a few household items I'm sure Jonathan has on hand. It's actually not that complicated. I'm surprised no one attempts it."

Connery growls low in his throat. *"No one attempts it because it puts the non-magic person at risk. She might go so far under tha she doesn't come back. Ye could kill her if you're not careful! Ye realize those are the stakes, right?"*

Bodhi's jaw tightens. "I wouldn't kill her. That's only happened once in the history books. That one story scared everyone so much that no one attempts it. But there are several other cases before that which worked perfectly fine. It merely transferred the cost of the magic to the lender, so the mage could do his thing." He locks his eyes on mine. "We don't have to do it. But if it's all on me, then we have to wait a few days before we hit another pharmacy. And we'll need a different exit strategy. Counting on me to get us out of there is asking to get caught."

I chew on my lower lip while I try to think up different possibilities that don't involve melding through a door.

I stand, knowing that I can't sacrifice my life for this cause. Seven needs me. I'm her only family left. After I took her in, that's when I started remembering to take multivitamins and get regular physicals. I have to keep myself healthy for her sake, otherwise she loses yet another parent.

"How many people died and how many people were just depleted in those studies you read about?"

Bodhi locks his eyes on mine. "One person died, eight people were depleted and recovered just fine."

"This has only been done nine times in history?"

Bodhi shrugs. "As far as I know."

I wait until Connery's maw is turned and then dive headfirst into a world in which I should not even dip my toe. "We'll have to find another way," I say aloud, but only Bodhi sees me mouth to him, *I'll do it.*

Bodhi's brows raise as he lifts his glass, saluting me with the protein shake. "We'll do it the way we did last time and hope for the best, then." But he winks at me, letting me know that the two of us have a secret.

A secret that has a one-in-nine chance of getting me killed.

20

VONDING WITH BODHI

*B*odhi and I don't mention a word of our unspoken agreement. I know that if Jonathan learned I was going to sacrifice myself like this, he would never stand for the second heist to happen.

But Bodhi and I have done a good job at staying on the same page, even though we haven't spoken a word about it since he laid out the details at the table, when both Connery and logic ruled out bonding myself to Bodhi.

But neither of those helpers are here now, sitting in the car, waiting the obligatory three minutes to be sure the coast is clear.

Bodhi pretended he needed the spices and herbs for a recipe he was going to make us tonight. And the red cord introduced itself covertly into the mix when I found a red shoelace of Jonathan's from his old pair of running sneakers and used it to tie back my hair. That's been my silent signal to Bodhi that I'm all in.

I really hope he has everything he needs for the vonding charm, otherwise I'm going to have to waterboard him yet again, and I'm not sure I have the stomach for it.

Or perhaps I do, which is even more troubling.

Jonathan steadies us all with an audible inhale and long exhale. "Okay, kids. I'll be right here. Same deal as last time. You do all the work; I drive the getaway car at a leisurely pace. Connery watches Seven back at home where she is far away from any of this."

That's Jonathan's way of telling me he doesn't like that he's the one staying behind while I do the heavy lifting with Bodhi.

I lean forward and kiss his cheek. "You're super fast and super furious. Better than old Vin Diesel himself." I tousle Jonathan's hair. "Plus, look at this head of hair. Absolutely luxurious. Stylish and helpful. That's you. Oh, and super dangerous."

Jonathan snickers at my teasing. "Yeah, yeah. Get going." He hands me a water bottle, knowing I'll need it to revive Bodhi.

Only hopefully, we won't need to do that this time.

Bodhi and I walk in step a few feet, letting the slightly cool air rouse and ready us for the task at hand. Then Bodhi does something strange. He pulls me to his side, his arm draped around my shoulders.

"Are we the friendly type?" I ask him with a skeptical

eye, the brim of my hat lifting to squint at him. "We're more criminal partners than anything else."

"Shush, love, and give me your finger."

I comply, only because I am too nervous about what we're going to do to argue.

I don't expect a prick of my finger, but when it happens, I suck in a gasp. "You could have warned me!"

"The blood has to be unwillingly given."

I blanch. "I'm liking this less and less the more I know about the whole thing."

"Fair point. Then don't ask questions. You're really not going to like this next part."

I close my eyes, praying for patience as we walk together. "Is the charm going to work? How worried do I need to be?"

"I'm in charge, pretty poppet. Worry needn't be part of your vocabulary."

I roll my eyes, grumbling under my breath just loud enough for him to hear my displeasure.

When we reach the backdoor, I make sure the brim of my baseball cap is tugged low enough to obscure my face, paired with a hoodie to hide my hair. "Let's do this." I hold tight to his elbow. "If anything should happen to me..."

"Yes, yes, you can feel free to haunt me as often as you like to make sure I'm helping Jonathan take care of Seven."

My shoulders lower a little, but the worry plagues me that I am making the wrong decision—valuing thousands of strangers' lives over my own daughter's.

Sweat beads on my upper lip.

No, that's not what I'm doing. Bodhi said it would be just fine. He is certain this won't kill me. If I really thought I would die, I wouldn't do this at all.

Bodhi takes a mini plastic container from his pocket that Jonathan uses for sauce leftovers, revealing a muddy liquid with plenty of chunks and mulch-looking speckles. He pops the top and angles my finger over the container, squeezing just enough to get one whole drop of blood to fall into the mix.

I don't expect anything to happen, so when the brown liquid turns a vibrant green, I gasp. "Should it be doing that?"

Bodhi grins excitedly, his eyes wide as he stares at his creation. "That's exactly what it should be doing. I'm telling you, if I die and it's to you to sing the song of my life, make sure to add in that I'm a devilishly handsome genius."

"I'll be sure to work up a jig that proclaims exactly that," I deadpan.

We stop in front of the back entrance to the largest pharmacy one county over from where we currently reside. This is even bigger than the first, so I have four duffels hooked over my shoulder.

"The red cord," Bodhi reminds me.

"Right. Here you go." I untie my hair with one hand, expecting this to be the end of my participation.

Bodhi holds me close, as if we're at the end of a date

that went very well. He turns so his body is flush to mine with my back to the door. The mixture of blood, spices and who knows what else is pressed between our bodies. He angles his neck toward me to whisper in my ear, "It works best if you don't resist. Actually, that's just my theory, not textbook wisdom, but I think it might help. Think about why you're doing this."

"Sheer terror? Coercion?" I joke. But then I soften when Bodhi fixes me with a stern look. "I'm doing this because your people deserve medicine. They deserve a chance to heal so they can stand up to the dictator whose ego is so fragile that he had to throw sick people in prison to secure his kingdom." I take in a long breath, letting my chest expand with the truth of what I believe. "I'm doing this because it's the right thing to do. I'm with you, Bodhi. I'm in this."

A man has not held me this close who was not Jonathan in a few years, and even Jonathan's hugs are few and far between because he knows this is too intimate for me. I haven't been on a date since before I adopted Seven, and even then, my girlfriend wasn't the snuggly type, which was fine by me.

While I know Bodhi is gay and this isn't romantic, it takes me some time to let my guard down. When my shoulders finally lower, Bodhi's thumb sweeps over the small of my back. "You're not one for closeness, are you."

"I don't like being held," I admit.

"And why is that?" he inquires, his forehead pressed to mine. I can feel his breath on my nose.

I shrug, but I know the answer. "It's too intimate. Too much. I'm afraid I'll feel things I've been trying not to touch, and they'll all come at me like a tidal wave and crush me. Then I won't be able to get out of bed in the morning and stand on my own. I need that—to be able to stand on my own."

Bodhi kisses the tip of my chilly nose. "I can respect that. We're going to stay just like this for a little while then, until you relax in my arms. I want to give this the best chance of success."

Panic climbs up my throat. "Then it's not going to work! I suck at this kind of thing."

"What kind of thing?"

I nearly squeak my anxiety when it comes out. "Intimacy! Raw affection. Closeness. Anything that means I have to relax in someone's arms."

Bodhi chuckles at my fretting. "I can be patient. You're a ball of anxiety even without the dreaded 'raw affection.' It makes sense that you don't deflate at the first touch." He kisses my nose again. "Close your eyes, love."

I harrumph and do as he requests, but I'm still tense and resistant, even though I want to be a team player.

"That's good. See? You trust me. You trust that I'm going to do all I can to return you to your daughter."

"It's not that." I grimace, my eyes still closed. "Well, it's not just that."

Bodhi's thumb soothes the base of my spine, unwinding a portion of my nerves and loosing my tongue just enough to be honest. "Then tell me, love. What is it that's got you twisted?"

Agony taints my tone. "You're holding me nicely."

"That's what's wrong? Would you rather I grip you like a man with anger issues? Because that's never been me. I'm not sure I could pull off the ruse."

"No, it's too nice. I'll cry if I let myself relax, which I know you need me to do for the spell to have its best chance of working."

Bodhi brushes his nose across mine, tender and sweet. "Tell me why you want to cry, love. Prostitutes make the best listeners, I assure you. You are safe with me."

I nod, knowing it's not him who is the problem. "I'll cry because... because it's hard. It's hard and it's heavy, and if I let myself feel that, I might not be able to be who I need to be to raise Seven. To get through the days."

Bodhi runs his hand across my cheek. "Darling," he coos. "I think it's time you let someone hold you when it's hard and it's heavy. Someone who will make sure you get through the days after you let yourself admit that sometimes life is hard—too hard to bear on your own."

"I might cry," I warn us both. "I don't want to do that."

"Shh," Bodhi says quietly, his arms curving around my back so there can be no mistaking the gesture.

This is it. This is a hug.

It's just as potent and frighteningly comforting as I thought it would be.

I let out a whimper, then muscle through the resistance I knew would come. This is fine. This is necessary.

In more ways than one.

He rocks me slowly, unhurried and unbothered at my emotional warts that might never fully heal. "Deep breaths together," he urges, waiting for me to comply.

Finally it comes. I breathe into the embrace enough that my forehead rests against the crook of his neck. I can smell the expensive body wash of Jonathan's that we've all been treating ourselves to. I can smell the pavement around us and the smattering of snow that adds a crispness to the night. I can smell the earthy scent of Bodhi beneath all that, and I use it to center myself, pushing out the panic so I can focus on the people.

My eyes shut tight as I use his neck like an oxygen mask, lowering my shoulders once again and handing Bodhi the small container of my blood, the herbs, and who knows what else. "I'm relaxed," I tell him, knowing this is as good as it's going to get. I'm not crying. I'm not freaking out.

I'm... I'm breathing.

I push my mind in the direction of Bodhi, recalling the tragic life he's lived and the altruistic streak that still wills him forward, braving death to save the people who did precious little to give him a leg up. There's something noble about it, something that wraps my arms around his torso, returning the hug in case his life has grown to hard and heavy for him to bear alone, too.

The red shoelace is dipped into the muddy liquid, then tied around our wrists—my left and his right. Bodhi holds me firmly to him, my chest married to his while he chants the words of the spell in a language I cannot decipher.

A chill moves over my skin, tripping down my spine and pushing me tighter into Bodhi's embrace. Though our feet are on solid concrete, it's beginning to feel as if we're on the edge of a cliff, and the only thing tethering us to the spot, so we don't topple over the edge, is each other.

I cling tighter to Bodhi, unwilling to fall into the abyss by myself. Unwilling to desert him to face this grave task alone.

The world goes dark around us, turning from midnight to absolute pitch black, devoid of even the streetlights. I want to ask him if this is supposed to happen, or if I have spontaneously gone blind, but I also don't want to interrupt his chant.

I close my eyes, so the darkness is my choice, rather than something that has been inflicted upon me. A whistling sound frightens me, but still, I remain silent.

It's only when the sky opens and sends down a deluge of rain out of nowhere that I make the smallest noise of fright.

There wasn't a forecast of rain for tonight, and

certainly not a flash flood so potent that the raindrops feel like tiny punches on my skin.

Bodhi keeps his chant going while he presses my back to the door, shielding me with his taller body so he takes the brunt of nature's beating. My hands fight to shield him as much as I am able. It's not that I'm afraid of him getting wet; it's that the rain is painful as it hurtles at us.

When a crack of thunder shakes the ground beneath my feet, I know nature did not plan on being this angry tonight.

We awakened her with magic, and now she is livid.

It's not until lighting hits the light in the parking lot behind us that I realize we are doing something we cannot take back.

21

ANGERING NATURE

*B*odhi and I are drenched to the skin, clinging to each other because even though we are adults, no child has ever been more frightened than we are now.

Or perhaps Bodhi is mildly shaken and I am the only one freaking out.

It's not until Bodhi holds our wrists aloft, showing Mother Nature the red shoelace soaked in a potion that intends to bind us together, that I realize what we are doing has an air of permanence to it.

I should resist, but I don't. I don't mind being bonded to someone who would do so much to right the wrongs inflicted upon those who cannot make themselves heard.

"Hold steady!" Bodhi warns me, dropping the potion on the concrete so he can wrap his free arm around my waist more securely. "Breathe with me! Together now!"

He has to shout over the noise of the rain that streaks over us.

When Bodhi's chest expands, so does mine. Together we fill our lungs with the cold, wet air, our bound hands over our heads and out to the side like we've been caught in a very strange dance.

The second peal of thunder rattles my teeth, but I keep my chest moving in time with Bodhi's.

It's the second strike of lightning I see as if in slow motion. The sky opens, sending a red streak zagging toward us. I don't have time to scream as the white-hot bolt shoots the motherload of electricity into our bound wrists, frying the red shoelace as if that's the thing for which the heavens were aiming.

I feel heat and smell something burning.

I grit my teeth through the pain, grateful that I am somehow alive and miraculously upright. That could be because Bodhi is holding me up, smooshing my body between his and the door.

I don't know if I am on fire, or if it's just the shoelace that's burning. I cry out, the sound muffled in Bodhi's collar. The heat builds so quickly; I worry that my hand might never recover. Nature rages around us, pelting us with water that mercifully drenches my arm, diluting the pain by degrees enough that I can breathe without screaming.

I haven't been afraid of a storm since I was a little girl. My mother swiftly informed me that being fearful was nothing more than childish nonsense, and she expected more from me. But tonight, I am that little girl, hiding under my bed and praying for daylight. All the steps that brought me to this moment in my life suddenly make no sense at all.

Except for the fact that people are dying from a curable disease, shunned by society because of something they contracted, not something horrible they did.

Maybe my actions weren't so irrational after all.

Bodhi leans forward, his body crushing me to the wall as our once bound hands drop to our sides. I'm no longer on fire, if that's what it was. The pain is a memory imprinted forever on my psyche, but luckily, it seems the worst has passed.

I whimper into Bodhi's shirt, grateful the darkness covers my quivering chin. He is shaking, his body upright by sheer force of will and a need to see this job through so he can liberate his people.

My uninjured hand reaches up and tangles in his hair, softening us both because we just went through a trauma and lived to tell the tale.

Only we cannot tell a soul about this. Jonathan doesn't play it fast and loose with my life, and it was clear that Connery was livid I even entertained the idea of permitting Bodhi to use me for the vonding charm.

"I'm sorry," Bodhi whispers, water dripping off his nose. "I'm sorry I put you through that. You have a child. It was so risky. I lost my way even asking you to do this. I'm so sorry, Zara. And please don't forgive me. That would only make it worse."

I don't know what to say to that. I'm mad at myself for not putting my own safety higher on the list. "Did it work? I really don't want to do that all again."

Bodhi presses his cheek to mine, only this time, I lean into the contact. There's a sweetness to it, a completion that makes no sense to me. Bodhi is gay, and while I'm bisexual, gay men are the one thing that do nothing for me, attraction-wise. So I know that's not what this is—this sigh of connection settling through me, as if touching his cheek is the only thing that feels right.

Which has to be wrong.

I'm tired. That must be what it is. And it's okay to feel connected to a person you have zero attraction to. But this tether is different than friendship. Different than love. It's... it's entirely other, so I lean into it, giving myself permission not to question every odd thing along the way. I was just struck by lightning, and I almost cried in front of a person. I'll take the comfort where I can find it.

"Let's see if it worked," Bodhi says quietly over the rain. Nature seems to be marginally less angry as it falls now, instead of purposefully pelting us.

I focus on Bodhi's cheek, and the odd calm that sedates the long list of worries I can never seem to escape.

The hug doesn't feel scary anymore.

In fact, it's kind of nice.

22

ROBBING THE PHARMACY

oving through the door is far simpler this time. We don't fall on the other side, and most surprising of all is that Bodhi is perfectly upright without a hint of fainting. It's as uneventful as if the door was open and we strolled right through it.

My mouth falls open in astonishment. "That's what it was supposed to do, right?"

Bodhi checks his torso, his arms, and then winces at the angry black and pink burn mark on his wrist. "I barely felt that. There was no drain on my magic at all. I could do it ten more times without a blink." His eyes zero in on me, his hands cupping my face with worry. "Are you alright? Should you sit down? I tapped into your lifeforce, so you should be as depleted as I was when we did this last time."

I check my faculties, surprised I feel no damage at all. "Other than my wrist, I don't feel a thing." I don't want to look at my arm. I don't want to see the scope of the damage.

I hand Bodhi a duffel bag, settling into task mode.

Bodhi is still marveling at the magic that made this all possible. I guess it's a major breakthrough that we are both upright after such an ordeal.

I don't want to think of the alternative, so I put myself to work.

This time, I tear the list in half, giving Bodhi the bottom part so we can divide and conquer.

The job goes so much quicker, now that there are two of us working, and I don't have to spend time water-boarding Bodhi to wake him. This pharmacy is larger, so we fill the four duffel bags easily, but there are still more antibiotics and steroids we could take.

"Give me the bags. I'll empty them in the trunk so we can fill them again," he whispers.

I expect him to need me near him when he moves through the doors, but he trots through effortlessly.

That time, however, I feel the wave of sickness you get when you know you're coming down with the flu. A nause-ating heat sweeps through me, doubling me over while I do my best not to vomit.

That one, I felt. That must be what sharing a lifeforce with Bodhi is like when he uses his magic and taps into my strength to do so when he's not physically touching me.

He's gone all of four minutes, which is enough time for

me to right myself and gather antibiotics into a pile so they're easier to stash when he returns. I also grab several months' worth of Jonathan's HIV medication, and more bottles of the puberty blockers that Seven will need in a few years.

Again, Bodhi trots through the closed door without a blink, but this time, the wave of sick brings me to my knees.

Bodhi swears and rushes to my side. His arm curves around my back, and immediately, the discomfort is gone.

I pant as I sag against him, relief rolling through my body. "I felt that one."

Bodhi kisses my temple, then tugs my hat down so my face is not seen by the cameras. "I'm so sorry, love. I'll only use my magic to get us out of here. I won't keep putting you through this. The bond will fade soon enough."

I nod, grateful for that.

He helps me to my feet so we can get back to work. I really hope this place has enough antibiotics that we don't have to hit another pharmacy. I hate that we're stealing. In fact, there's not a ton about my new undead life that I'm all that thrilled about.

Maybe now that I'm presumed dead, I'm a thief, but only a very specific type of burglar. I only steal medication to give to the disenfranchised.

Somehow this soothes my conscience enough to keep my hands moving and my feet pointed toward their purpose.

Bodhi and I waste no time at all. We work together like a seamless ballet, filling the duffels with our movements in sync as we search the shelves for everything on our lists.

We're nearly finished when the sound of a keypad's buttons being pushed shoots fear through my spine. As careful as we've tried to be, somehow we've been found out.

23

INTRUDERS

odhi is still new to my world, so the sound inflicts curiosity in him rather than panic.

"Bodhi, hide!" I whisper, pointing toward the exit.

There aren't many places to slip out of view that are foolproof. The entire storage area is a series of shelves with tiny bottles and boxes lining them, which hardly provides proper cover.

Bodhi rushes to me so we can hide together, which I'm not sure is the best idea. The pills rattle in their bottles, surely ratting us out the moment the door opens.

"Be absolutely silent," Bodhi warns me, holding my hand. "There's a spell to turn myself invisible, but I'm really bad at it. I've actually never done it successfully before."

"Oh, that's a relief!" I spout off sarcastically.

His hand goes over my mouth. "But even if I pull it off,

I can't keep the medicine silent when it jostles." He locks his eyes on mine in the darkness lit only by the glow of the red emergency exit light. "I have to tap into you again."

"Do it!" Darn his good manners. "Just get us out!"

The door opens and the overhead lights go on. "I'm telling you, the cameras picked up two people breaking in during the flash flood," a man's voice says.

I'm sweating, certain the rest of my undead life will be spent behind bars, and everyone in those Crimshade prisons will continue to wither away.

Bodhi presses his finger to his lips, reminding me that while he might be able to turn us invisible (heavy on the "might"), he cannot make us inaudible.

Which is going to be a problem the second we try to move.

"I don't see anyone," says the other voice. "And the alarm wasn't triggered. Are you certain that's what you saw?"

"Of course that's what I saw! I showed you the footage."

The second man sighs. "All I saw was two teenagers making out behind the building, which is hardly worth us coming here in the middle of the night to investigate."

I straighten a little, accepting the compliment that the shadowy silhouette of me can pass for a teenager.

"They're in here. Maybe they know the code for the keypad."

"The storm shorted the footage. They disappeared on

the camera because they probably went to go find a less rainy spot to make out."

Part of me silently corrects the assumption that Bodhi and I were smooching, but because he referred to me as a teenager, I let it slide. I don't get that compliment often, now that I'm thirty-three.

I wait for the wave of sick to come over me, informing me that I'm now invisible from Bodhi tapping into my life-force and casting his invisibility spell over us, but the nausea never comes. Still, Bodhi holds my hand, walking us silently toward the door with the two men none the wiser. Bodhi is sweating, or maybe it's my palm that's clammy. I pray that the bottles don't rattle too noticeably as we place one foot in front of the other, stepping out in plain view.

Panic wells in my throat when one of the men turns and looks straight at me. I wait for him to call the police and start shouting, but he turns and goes about the business of looking for two hoodlums boning in the backroom of the pharmacy.

Maybe Bodhi actually pulled it off.

The urge to run is strong, but we keep a steady snail's pace until we reach the exit. This time, we have the option of opening the door, but that would alert the two that something is amiss.

Through the solid surface it is. I plaster my back to the door, closing my eyes because in my mind, that's me helping. I try to block out the fretting I can hear from the two men, now that they realize they've been robbed.

"Call the police! I knew the break-in at the other pharmacy wasn't a one-time hit!"

Bodhi wastes no time pushing us through the closed door. I don't experience the flu-like nausea I had earlier, so perhaps Bodhi is just getting better at this whole thing.

Better at stealing.

Like me.

Once the night air kisses our cheeks, we break into a run, bolting toward the car while still holding onto each other. I throw myself into the passenger's seat, shaking with nerves until Jonathan drives away from the scene of the crime at a leisurely pace.

"Do I want the recap?" Jonathan asks me, his hands gripping the steering wheel as he drives five miles below the speed limit.

"Nope," Bodhi and I reply together.

"You both okay?"

"Yep," comes our succinct response. Though it's clear we are anything but.

Jonathan reaches over and squeezes my hand—a thing he only does when he's mired in worry. "That was our last heist," he rules, quiet but firm. "You both were nearly caught."

I don't have any arguments for him because I'm leaning the same way.

Jonathan glances in the rearview mirror at Bodhi. "You

don't look like you're one sneeze away from death. Was the backdoor opened or something? Did you not have to use your magic?"

Bodhi runs his hand through his inky hair. "I suppose I'm just getting better at this new life of crime."

Jonathan doesn't buy that non-explanation in the least, but fortunately, he doesn't press for more details.

"It's done," I say just above a whisper. "That'll have to do for now."

"Forever," Jonathan rules. He squeezes my hand again, reminding me that I am not alone in this world. My best friend is here to make sure I don't fall over the edge of sanity and do something I can't take back.

I don't know how I got so lucky. I can only hope my brand-new streak of fortune doesn't run out.

24

TWO SOLDIERS

When we pull onto Jonathan's street, a figure catches my eye. It's not uncommon to see people out walking their dogs or going for a run during the day, but in the dead of night, the two men standing under the streetlamp looks out of place.

"Leather armor," I say aloud when we get closer.

Bodhi swears. "Jonathan, turn around and take us away from the house. Those are the king's soldiers. If they're here, it means they've found Connery, and they're not going to be pleased to see that I'm still alive."

Anxiety shoots through my veins. "Seven! We have to get her out! They'll blow up Jonathan's home just like they did mine!"

Bodhi leans forward, eyeing Jonathan's place in the distance. "I don't see a massacre, and if I'm not mistaken... I can't tell who the taller one is, but the squat one is

Beneen. Soldiers in general love to put on a good show to display their favor with the king, but those two are guilty of that in particular. And they're far more skilled than many of their colleagues."

Panic rips through me, spiking my heartrate. "I'm not leaving my daughter unprotected, and I'm not letting them take Connery! If they want a show, I'll give them a show." Though I'm tired, unskilled, and unarmed, I would rather die than leave my little girl.

Jonathan is of the same mind. "Zara, you run in and grab Connery and Seven. Get them in the car as fast as you can. Bodhi and I will keep the soldiers busy."

I hate the idea of leaving Jonathan's side mid-crisis, but it's the smartest way to get us all out.

Bodhi reaches his hand forward and cups my shoulder. "I might need to..." He doesn't finish his request because Jonathan's not supposed to know that he can tap into my lifeforce.

I cover Bodhi's fingers with mine. "Do whatever you need to. Just get us all out alive."

Bodhi squeezes my shoulder, then thumbs my cheek. That small affection sinks into my heart and settles the bits that are banging around, asking for a home where they can rest.

Though I barely know him, Bodhi's touch is that home for my heart.

I really hate that. He hasn't earned the right to settle

my unrest that easily, yet some physiological part of me calms at his touch.

That can't be right.

I don't understand it, but this is hardly the time for a deconstruction of magical theory. Jonathan parks the car in the driveway and shoves the keys into my hand. "Quick!"

I race out of the car, jam the key into the lock and throw open the front door. "Connery!" I shout through the condo that is lit only by a lamp in the living room.

My dog trots to me, eyes lidded. I can tell I woke him up.

"Connery, Bodhi's in trouble! There are two soldiers outside. We have to get out of here now! I'll grab Seven. You go help the guys."

Connery is wide awake now. He darts out of the house while I run to Jonathan's bedroom to retrieve my baby angel.

Thankfully, she sleeps like the dead, so I am able to scoop her up without rousing her.

I run her to the front door, but before I reach it, the living room window to my right shatters, blasting glass inward and all over us. I turn to the side in hopes that Seven is shielded from the brunt of the attack.

Horror and shock pelt me along with the glass, informing me that nothing that should be safe in fact, is. Seven and I shriek in surprise mingled with pain. I don't know why I thought I would be able to get her out of the house and to safety in time to escape whatever wrath is exploding in on us.

I shield my baby angel as much as humanly possible. I scream as more glass shards pepper my arms and back with the splintering of the window to the left of the door.

Seven's screams turn the blood in my veins to ice.

I was supposed to protect her. I was supposed to raise her.

This wasn't supposed to happen.

I barrel out of the house with Seven tight in my arms, unsure if the car is our safety point, or if I should have turned tail and run out the backdoor. I race out into the night, terrified when the first thing I hear is the gurgling cry of a man.

I can only pray it isn't Jonathan. Not Jonathan. He's given up so much to help us. I know being my best friend is the thing that holds him back.

And now it's the thing destroying his home.

I shove Seven into the backseat of my car, scared that whatever she is seeing, it is too adult for little eyes. "Keep your head down, Sev. Make yourself as small as possible."

It's the one piece of advice I swore I would never give her. I raised her to take up space in the world, no matter how many people and policies wanted to shut her up and keep her invisible, so they didn't have to acknowledge that no, they are not in charge of anyone's body but their own.

Still, I motion to the floor, where she folds her knees to her chest obediently.

I slam the door shut and do what I can to make myself useful in the fight against the two soldiers. I'm not exactly sure how, but I'm ready to tackle someone.

When I round the car to take in the sight unfolding on the front lawn, my jaw drops open at what I certainly never expected I might see.

Connery is tearing the throat out of one of our attackers. The squat one named Beneen, I think. Sinew and blood drip from his maw. He growls as if he was always meant to be this wild, protecting us with a vengeance that knows no mercy.

The felled soldier's eyes are lifelessly staring into the night as Connery takes another bite, tearing an artery that spits blood at his face.

Jonathan doubles over, heaving as if he is seconds away from losing his dinner on the lawn.

I am not far behind.

Bodhi stares at his hands with a mix of fear and wonder. He's trembling on the other side of the car, backing up slowly as if he is being threatened to stand down. "What have I done? What have I done?"

But the soldier who isn't being feasted on by Connery doesn't appear to be the least bit threatening. He's got his arms raised in surrender, his chin angled downward in total submission. "I'm not here to attack you!" the man declares.

Connery's voice vibrates through the air. *"Well, this one did. He comes on our property, he dies."*

I've never heard that sort of authoritative talk from my sweet pup. I knew he was controlled by Highbron, the king's mage, to carry out all sorts of unsavory deeds, but I didn't dream he would have the wherewithal to conjure aggression without Highbron's prodding. Connery's so precious and cuddly (when blood isn't dripping from his maw).

The man on his knees on the grass still has his hands up. "Tell your mage to stand down, Captain! I'm not here to bring you in."

Bodhi looks positively frightened of himself. Perhaps it was him who blasted out the windows in an attempt to take out the intruders. He stands on shaking legs to confront the man on the grass. "You have no ill intention? I find that hard to believe. You came here in your armor, and I know there's a price on Connery's head. You won't take my best friend from me! No one will take him ever again!" Bodhi extends his arms ominously, so I step back, unsure what the right move is. I can see the fear mingled with his rage, the worry that he will once again be the lonely boy in the orphanage without his friend to look out for him.

"Stand down, Bodhi," Connery growls.

I can tell by Bodhi's clenched jaw that he does not like this command in the slightest, yet he complies, lowering his arms. But I can tell he's not ready to call the fight over.

I rush to Bodhi's side. "You want to live? Then talk.

Connery might want to spare your life, but this is the one who needs convincing." I jerk my thumb to Bodhi.

The man whimpers. "I'm Pavma. Pavma Lakshi of the Green Battalion, third rank."

I feel like I've heard Connery say this man's name before, but I can't recall the conversation.

Connery offers a succinct, *"Pavma is the one who helped me escape the castle. He's the one who helped shatter the emerald tha held my will."*

Well, that makes a giant difference. Relief flickers through my nervous system, but Bodhi remains tensed at my side.

Pavma's eyes dart to Connery. "Highbron took over in your stead."

Connery growls. *"The king's mage knows nothing of being a soldier. All Highbron knows is magic and greed."*

Pavma nods. "Oh, it's far worse than you could imagine. When you escaped, Highbron named himself commander of the king's army. It's nothing like when you were in charge. There was order. There was a system you trained us to follow. When you were labeled disloyal, no one knew what to believe or what it is we're doing. You were the most loyal to King Artifice because you had no choice! When you came down with the traitor's disease..." Pavma shakes his head, swallowing hard. "So many laid down their swords, but they were quickly slaughtered on Highbron's command. I still serve the throne because the only alternative is death, and I can't be useful to the people if I'm dead."

Pavma motions to his deceased countryman on the grass. "There are men like him, who do all they can with the same zeal they've always had for the throne, but the ones like me are dying as soon as our loyalties are made known. So I keep my head down, following the rules without knowing the point of any of it anymore. I had to get to you, Connery. I had to go on this mission to find you because the orders are to kill you." He motions to the lamppost where we saw him when we drove home. "Why do you think I was standing in plain sight? I wanted you to see us, so you'd have a chance to escape." He shouts to Bodhi, who still looks ready to attack, "Connery knows where I stand!"

Bodhi turns to his best friend. "Connery?"

Connery nods once, indicating that Pavma can be trusted. Then Connery slashes his paw across the dead man's face just to be cruel.

"Connery!" I scold him, though I know I should keep my mouth shut.

My dog's head bows like a scolded pup.

"That's just plain gratuitous. He's dead enough. No need to be gross about it." I move my hands to my hips, but grimace when I start to feel the dozens of shards of glass across my back and arms. I think I must've blocked out the pain of it all in the hullabaloo. Now that we're at a standstill, I am very aware that my back is bleeding in several spots.

Connery rushes to me, lapping my body three times to

survey the damage. I hear a panicked whine in his throat. It shifts to a command when he turns to the soldier. *"Pavma can help ye. He's bandaged up many a soldier in his day."*

"Yes, ma'am." Pavma nods enthusiastically. He looks to be in his mid-forties or perhaps fifty years old.

Connery eyes Pavma and jerks his head toward me. *"This is my m'dolla. Zara was injured from the blast. She has deep cuts tha need tending to. Can ye give them a look?"*

Pavma's mouth falls open in time with Bodhi's. "She's your *what*?" Bodhi screeches, his brows raised. Whatever Connery just called me, Bodhi has opinions about it.

Maybe I should too. And I would if I knew what it meant, or if I wasn't mid-fright.

Pavma remains on his knees, locking his fingers behind his head in complete submission. His furtive glances in my direction flit away quickly but keep returning, as if he can't believe I exist.

Which is weird because all I'm doing is standing here, bleeding.

I'm bleeding.

A swoon of fear swoops over me, coupled with a crash of adrenaline, now that it seems the worst of the danger is behind us.

My gaze falls on Connery, who trots over to sniff his kill, looking like the predator he was born to be. "Can we trust him?"

Connery dips his head. *"I do. But I'll watch him until ye trust him."*

It's a solid answer, giving me the space to embrace my wariness instead of being forced into blind acceptance of this whole thing.

PAVMA

When Pavma slowly stands and steps toward me, I shake my head. "Seven first. I don't know if she was cut. I tried to shield her, but I don't know how great a job I did."

Bodhi comes to life, trotting to the car and opening the backdoor. "It's safe for you to come out now, wee Petunia. But only if you promise to close your eyes until we get inside."

Jonathan and I rush to the backseat, going into parent-mode. My demeanor shifts because fear is not what my daughter needs in this moment. A tender smile crosses my face. "Come here, Princess."

When she steps out of the car in her pajamas, I can see tears glistening off her cheeks in the moonlight, her eyes scrunched shut.

"Baby!" I coo, picking her up, swallowing a gasp when

her pajama snags on one of the shards of glass sticking out of my arm. I slowly walk her into Jonathan's condo, fighting a wince so I don't show her how badly my back and arms hurt. "Are you okay, sweetie?"

Seven's lower lip quivers as she holds up her finger. "I got blooded!"

It's her way of telling me she's been cut.

Jonathan's face pulls, his own panic ebbing now that he has to be the father. "Oh, no! How about Mommy takes you inside to get a better look at it." He keeps his body between her and the dead soldier as much as possible, so she doesn't see just how grim this Crimshade life can get.

I take her to the bathroom and sit her on the lid of the toilet, rummaging in Jonathan's medicine cabinet for Band-Aids and antibacterial cream.

But when Seven catches a glimpse of my cuts, she gasps. "Mommy, no!"

I locate a smile in the recesses of my brain just for her. "I'm sure it looks worse than it is. I'm completely fine. Let's see to that hand of yours. I think Papa Jonathan has just the thing in here."

He has so many pills to keep his HIV from becoming detectible. I'm grateful he has access to them, but looking at them all breaks my heart. I don't want anything to hurt him ever; he's too pure and perfect.

I also don't want my baby to have a cut on her finger, yet here we are.

I make sure no glass is stuck in her skin and then

cleanse the area that is no bigger than a papercut on her knuckle, thank goodness.

"All better?" Jonathan asks as he appears in the doorway of the bathroom, his expression falsely composed.

Seven nods, swallowing back the last of her tears.

Jonathan jerks his head toward the hallway. "I want you to go straight to my bed and lie down. It's still nighttime, and I don't want you near the mess out here."

Seven tiptoes to him and raises her arms, silently begging to be held.

Jonathan melts for her, which is one of the things that makes him such a fantastic father. She is his world, which is something every little girl deserves. "That was scary, huh."

Seven sniffles into his cheek. "So scary."

Jonathan smooches her and then sets her back down. "To bed with you. I need to have a chat with Mommy."

I cringe, knowing what he's going to say once there are no little ears listening in.

As soon as Seven shuts herself in Jonathan's bedroom, his face turns grave as he fixes me with a cautious stare. "This is getting out of control," he says quietly to me.

"I know." I swallow hard, keeping my eyes on the Band-Aids as I put them back in the cabinet. "Give Pavma time to deal with my cuts, and we'll go. I'll find a way to replace the broken window and I'll send you the money once I do."

Jonathan's face sours. "I don't want money. Why would you say that?"

I blink at him standing there, his visage filling the doorway. "Because you're tapping out. You need us to leave because this is all getting too dangerous. I don't blame you."

"It's too dangerous for a seven-year-old," he clarifies. "She can't go with us to Crimshade, and you know it. We have to make a better plan than just going along with the chaos and hoping nothing hits us."

My lower lip quivers. "I have no plan!" I whisper-shout, not wanting Seven to catch the distress I constantly feel.

Jonathan reaches out and holds my undamaged hand. "Bodhi and Connery can take the medicine to Crimshade without us, is all I'm saying. You, Seven, and me are going to stay here. We don't need to see this thing through to the end. We did our part, and now it's time to let the Crimshade crew go. Let them return to their mess while we deal with cleaning up ours."

"You're not kicking us out?" I ask, confused and on the edge of letting too much emotion show.

Jonathan's face sours. "Of course not."

I nearly collapse against him, relieved that I am not too much for my best friend. I don't often hug Jonathan but being so near Bodhi during the heist knocked something loose in me.

Jonathan is just as surprised as I am that I'm leaning into him. "Whoa! Easy, Zara. It's alright."

But when his arms curve around me, I shriek in pain that I did not see coming.

How much glass is in my back? I've been trying to block it all out, but the pain is charging at me a mile a minute now that the worst of the danger is hopefully behind us.

Jonathan jumps back, his hands raised. "I'm sorry!" He turns his head at the sound of a tiny sniffle and lowers his shoulders. "Hey, I thought I told you to go lie down. What happened to that?"

Seven mumbles through an excuse that measures out to needing to hear the bedtime song again, or she won't be able to rest.

Jonathan turns toward the front of the home. "Bodhi, I'm going to put Seven back to sleep. Can you sweep up the glass? And Connery, I need you to watch the new guy like a hawk, you hear?"

That's Boss Jonathan, who gives orders in a measured way and isn't afraid to take charge of a room, no matter how messy.

"I love you," I whisper.

Jonathan smirks, despite the gravity of the situation. "You'd better." He angles his head to smile at our girl. "Who's got two thumbs and wants a bedtime story in the big bed?"

Seven beelines to him, holding up her finger. "But you have to carry me. I have an injury." Her Bambi eyes milk him for all he's worth. "I got blooded."

Jonathan feigns horror as he walks with her down the hall. "You got blooded? You're so brave. I think that deserves two stories. With voices."

"Oo! Can you do the fancy one?"

"Only the fanciest, and only for you."

My gosh, I love them.

I come out of the bathroom with antiseptic in my hands, gauze, and very little hope that this will do. My back hurts and it's sticky with a mixture of sweat and blood, which can't be good.

Bodhi is sweeping up the glass in the living room while Connery sits beside Pavma, who is standing with his hands locked behind his head so as not to spook any of us with his presence. Now that Pavma is here in the light of the living room, I can get a better look at him.

Black hair, brown skin like mine, rounded chin, and downcast eyes. Apart from the leather armor, Pavma doesn't look threatening, though his bulk is akin to Jonathan's, so I'm sure that verdict could change on a dime. When he glances up at me cautiously, there is a worn quality to his features, like he's been on the verge of calling it quits for a long time, despite that the only way out of the army seems to be death.

My heart tugs, my intuition informing me that I don't need to be on my guard around Pavma.

Or maybe my nervous system is too exhausted to hold onto even the smallest bit of angst this late at night, so it surrenders with a shrug.

Connery licks my fingers. *"I'll watch him,"* he assures me in his thick brogue.

My fingers tremble as I survey the damage that used to be Jonathan's pristine, stain-free living room. No one speaks as Connery nudges me toward the kitchen so I can sit in one of the chairs at the table under the light.

Bodhi watches Pavma's every move from his spot near the dust pan, though it's clear to me that the poor guy wanted out of soldier duties long ago. Pavma's hands tremble as he surveys my arm with the tweezers I found in the cabinet poised in his hand. "I'm sorry," he begins. "But we have to get this off you if I'm to deal with the glass." He casts Connery an apologetic look.

"No sweat," I assure them both. Pavma reaches out to help, but I bite my lip through a scream when I tug at the hem and quickly peel my shirt up over my head, then puddle it on the floor. I don't particularly like being this exposed to the stranger, but I don't have much of a choice.

Pavma's eyes focus only on the work, rather than the woman in a bra and jeans sitting at the table, straddling a chair, and trying to appear nonchalant.

"Hey," I tell Pavma quietly when his hands shake. "It's going to be okay. Thanks for doing this."

Pavma does not take courage from my words. "Forgive me, but if I make one mistake, the captain will have my head."

I frown over my shoulder at Connery who, sure

enough, looks ready for his second murder of the night. "Nah. Connery is a sweetheart."

Pavma snorts, then covers the indiscretion with a quick apology.

Connery whines at my near nakedness, but he doesn't throw a fit because we need Pavma to dig the glass out of my skin.

"You're doing a good job," I tell Pavma as he pulls a piece of glass from my shoulder. "I'm Zara."

Pavma nods, his eyes on his work. He uses tweezers to pluck the glass out of my arm, then covers the bloody splotch with a washcloth so I don't have to see the cut. It's all very humane, and if not for the fact that we are completely new to each other, I bet I would feel completely at ease around Pavma, who doesn't seem to have an agenda other than being helpful.

My shoulders relax as I slump on the chair, grateful that, at least for now, we have one more person on our side.

CONNERY'S DUTY AND MINE

Bodhi works on the front room, sweeping up the glass. Then he takes cardboard boxes from the recycling so he can patch the hole for the time being with a roll of duct tape.

When Pavma focuses the tweezers on my back, Connery's current of frustration turns him into pure puppy. He doesn't like that I'm hurt, and neither do I. Instead of glaring at Pavma while he works, Connery moves to my side, resting his throat and maw over my leg.

My hand reaches down to stroke his fur. I can feel the vibrations of his worry sinking into my thigh, trusting me to hold his fear for safe keeping.

I love him so much. To be loved by a dog? It's just about the best feeling in the world.

"I didn't hesitate," Connery tells me quietly. *"I tore out tha lad's throat without a blink."*

"You saved us," I agree, my fingers feathering the felt of his ear. I wince when Pavma digs out a particularly troublesome shard of glass from my back.

"I've never killed anyone without Highbron calling the shots."

I purse my lips, and instead of arguing the necessity of his actions, I let him feel what he needs to feel without tempering his words. It seems that even though Connery is not in Crimshade anymore, he hasn't left his soldier life completely behind.

It might be the sort of thing that's engrained too deep to let go.

I take my time stroking his fur, trying not to tense up when Pavma has to dig out a particularly deep shard of glass. "It's okay," I coo to my dog, running the velvet of his other ear between my fingers. "Everything's going to be okay."

Though my encouragement is meant for Pavma and Connery, I need to hear the mantra as well. "It's going to be okay," I repeat quietly. Then I let my imagination breathe in the fresh air, instead of keeping her trapped and gagged behind my logic. "We can start over. Move somewhere that isn't so happy to hate trans children and the scary people who raise them." My hand ruffles through Connery's fur. "A place with a big backyard for you. Three bedrooms, so Jonathan and Bodhi can come to visit whenever they like, and there will be a guest room waiting for them." My vulnerability peeks through my veil of parental responsibility. "Maybe there can be an apple tree, where we can eat apples right off the branches. Flowers in the front yard, even though I have a black thumb. But maybe in my new life, I'll take the time to learn how to garden. Maybe my new life will always have flowers." A soft smile sweeps over my face. "I could get Seven one of those canopy beds with the curtains that make you feel like a legit princess. She would love that."

Connery closes his eyes, as if my dreams are painful to him. Or maybe he's upset he can't make them come true.

But I can. I know my stubborn streak is the best weapon I have in my fight against the quicksand of life.

"I can't go with you to Crimshade," I tell Connery quietly. "I have a daughter who shouldn't be anywhere near a vicious dictator."

Connery nuzzles his head into my side. *"I can't leave ye behind. I won't."*

"You're going to have to. Go heal your people in the prisons, then come visit me when you can. That is, if you want," I quickly amend, careful never to give him anything that sounds like a directive.

I really hope he wants to come back to us. I didn't realize how badly my heart needed a companion like Connery. I don't feel nervous talking to him about my shortcomings. I don't hold myself back as much as I do with everyone else.

Pavma stills, speaking for the first time with curiosity rather than fear. "Heal the people in our prisons? That's not possible. It's a nice thought, though. Connery, I can see why you're so very protective of her. Optimism is in short supply these days."

I try to keep my voice steady while Pavma plucks glass from my back. "My world has the medicine that can cure the traitor's disease. Bodhi and Connery are already taking it. They're both about a week and a half away from being cured. Their skin lesions will take longer, but they'll heal well enough, hopefully without too much scarring."

Pavma stills. While I can't see his face because my back is to him, I can tell he is shaken to his core. "It's not possible. There is no cure. We know it's not true that only traitors to the throne come down with the sickness. That myth was debunked when Captain Connery contracted it. He was the most loyal to the throne because he had no choice. When word spread that he was diseased, there was a revolt. Many soldiers left the king's army—all without their heads."

"That's horrible," I offer.

Pavma returns to working on my back. "I stayed in the king's army because I hoped to change the tides from the inside. Plus, soldiers were being sent to Common to search for you, Captain. I wanted to be the one to find you, so I could save your life instead of the capture and kill I've been ordered to do."

"Ye did stab your fellow soldier," Connery says in astonishment. *"I wasn't sure I saw what I saw, but tha's why Beneen was so easy to kill. Ye stabbed him in the side."*

Pavma pauses before confirming the sin. "I had to. He wasn't going to take you in. Most of the soldiers who stayed are out for blood when it comes to traitors to the throne. They want to prove their loyalty to the king with how much blood they spill. The lust for violence grows daily, taking over reason and humanity until those treasures are a mere memory."

The silence spreads out while Pavma's words sink in.

Connery trusts Pavma, so that helps me breathe easier around him.

Connery licks my fingers. *"I need to deliver the medicine to the prisoners, but then I'll be returning to my m'dolla."*

Pavma moves slower over my back, his fingers slick with my blood. "You have a true weakness now. One that cannot be cured." His tone turns grave. "You cannot let it be known your heart lies with her. The soldiers who stayed hate you the most. They will come for Zara to cut your heart out if they cannot best you, and they will not be merciful in her death."

My blood feels like ice in my veins. "I'd be in danger because Connery is my dog?"

Pavma's voice comes back with a smirk to it. "Is that what you call the most fearsome captain the kingdom of Crimshade has ever known? Your dog? Soldiers have been beheaded for such disrespect. Highbron commanded Connery, and Connery commanded us. His word was law because his word was the king's."

My brows furrow. "Look, whatever is happening in

your world, just make sure it stays contained to Crimshade. As far as I know, only you and Bodhi know that Connery is my dog. No one is going to find out unless you or Bodhi talk, which it doesn't sound like you're going to if you're warning us to keep a lid on it. What I don't understand is why. Why would anyone care that Connery has a family now?"

Connery's tail hooks around my leg. I can tell he likes the idea of being in our family.

Pavma's voice turns grave once again. "Because Connery's owner is supposed to be the king. Connery was the king's righthand until the disease took him over. He is not allowed a love other than the will of King Artifice. The king does not share loyalties."

My jaw drops in horror as the sick way of their world washes over me. "What an insecure little man," I say with a snarl. "You're not going back there, Connery. Not if Artifice is as psychotic as you say. You'll never make it back alive."

Connery speaks slowly to me, his maw buried in my abdomen. *"I have to cure the ones I incarcerated. They are at the king's mercy because of me, and the king has none to give them. This is my penance, and if I must pay with my life, frankly, I understand tha fate would ask it of me."*

Pavma moves from behind me to address Connery. "Right there. That's why I would follow you to the grave and beyond. You didn't gloat or make the arrests violent if at all possible. You did the job without becoming a monster. I know what it is to be stuck while you're sinking in self-loathing and regret." He bows his head, his hands pressed together in front of his heart. "You do not have an army behind you anymore, but you have one soldier who truly believes we should all be free. If you can heal the prisoners, I will go with you into the prisons to deliver the medicine. You will always be my captain. I will follow you until the end. Your m'dolla is my queen."

My eyes widen with shock, and I realize I am in way over my head.

Connery straightens, nodding his head once to accept this man's fealty. *"Then into the prison we'll go. If we make it out alive, I'll have ye to thank."*

I jerk my thumb to my back. "Can I be done now? Is it finished? I need to disconnect from this for one entire night of sleep. I'm all turned around, and I just want to be done."

"Almost." Pavma returns to his work, picking out the last few pieces from my arms before he dumps antiseptic over the cuts. The pain sizzles on my skin, causing me to tense up and grip the back of the chair on which my chin is resting. Connery doesn't like when I'm in pain, so I try to keep the theatrics to a minimum.

Pavma wraps my torso with a stretchy bandage, keeping his eyes on his work in a clinical way, even though I am topless.

Connery goes into Jonathan's bedroom and returns

with one of my bestie's gym shirts, so I have something to wear that isn't stained with my blood.

"I need sleep," I tell them both. "Sleep and not this." I incline my head to Pavma. "Thank you for fixing me up. Though, you did break the window in the first place, so how about we call it even?"

Pavma's nose scrunches. "That wasn't my doing or Beneen's. It was someone on your end. I assumed it was the mage, but I recognize him, so I'm not sure that was his doing. Bodhi is barely a notch above us regular folk; he hardly has any magic, and certainly not enough to blow out those windows." Pavma glances from me to Connery, who I can tell doesn't care for talk about Bodhi that implies he's not the super best at everything.

Gotta love the loyalty of those two.

Then who broke the windows?

Connery trots into the living room to survey the damage, trying to piece together how the window blasted so potently when the attack didn't come from the soldiers.

I don't want a thing to do with getting to the bottom of anything. I'm a thousand pounds of tired, and I have no peace at all about what will need to happen in the morning. "No one else is coming for us?" I ask Pavma quietly.

He presses his hand to his chest in solemn vow. "On my honor, we are the only ones who came to hunt down Connery this round. Until I saw Connery with my own eyes, I thought him dead. It might be the best weapon he has at his disposal—the presumption of his death. Now no one is coming to take him back to be sentenced."

I swallow hard. Part of me wants to leave this conversation and get some sleep. The other part of me needs to know how much danger Connery is in. "Sentenced?"

Pavma lowers his chin. "He would be lucky to rot in the king's prison. It's widespread that if Connery is found, he is to be brought in for a public beheading. He was the king's most loyal servant. His righthand. The king doesn't trust easily, and now that the trust is breached, what with Connery coming down with the traitor's disease and getting his will back, the king will never forgive Connery for tempting him into trust."

My stomach hollows. "Then Connery can't go back to your world to deliver the medicine to your people. If he'll be killed, the medicine won't reach the prison in the first place."

Pavma's expression is grave. "I will do whatever it takes to bring the medicine to the people who need it, but I am only one soldier. I'm afraid I don't know how to help my own people." His jaw tightens. "I have failed."

I don't know Pavma, not really. Whether I should trust him or not isn't something I am willing to waste my time debating. The skepticism and worry that comes from being on my guard all the time now that I'm a parent drifts away, leaving me with the softer self I always worry I've sacrificed to adulthood.

I see this man's devastation, his dreams dashed, and his soul crushed.

I also see that it was a soul worth saving, because he's not even crushed for selfish reasons. He is crushed because his people will die, and he cannot help them.

Though I do not know Pavma well, I close the gap between us and hold onto his hand. "I'm sorry this is going so horribly. It's like we get one step closer to helping them, and there's a brick wall every time that we can't bypass."

Pavma freezes at the contact. It's like he's never had a gesture of kindness before in his life. Or perhaps it's been so long since I've held a man's hand that I've forgotten how and I'm doing it wrong. Is that possible?

I drop his hand in the next breath, then mumble any excuse for an exit. I move toward the bathroom so I can at least wash my face and pretend this whole night is something I can sleep off.

I lock the door behind me and splash water on my face, wishing life could be simpler.

Though, that's nothing new. I'm pretty sure I always wish that.

Now that I'm finally by myself in the bathroom, I can be alone with my worry, my anxiety, and my grief.

I watched a man die tonight.

I stole tens of thousands of dollars' worth of medicine. Again.

I'm about to lose my dog to duty.

I slink down and sit on the bathroom floor, pulling my

legs up to my chest. The cuts on my back are uncomfortable, but I need to hide from the mirror because I don't want to see myself cry, and I am dangerously close.

I can't fall apart right now—or ever, really.

Strong emotions war with my resolve, battling to see which will take over and call the shots.

When a knock sounds at the door, I wish for an eternity of space where I can be alone with no responsibilities or fears.

But that's not reality, so I stand and make sure I don't look like I was close to crying.

Jonathan is waiting for me outside the bathroom, no doubt knowing with his sixth sense that I'm on the verge of a breakdown. "Everything is a mess," I confess to him, though he already knows as much. It's not exactly a greeting, but it's all I've got.

Jonathan's shoulders lower with compassion, his head tilting to the side. "Then it's a mess for another day. You can't solve it all in a night, Zara. You're getting some sleep, then we'll tackle it all in the morning."

I want to protest on principle alone, not wanting to leave things unsolved, but I know I'm tapped. If I want to keep up with Seven tomorrow, I'll need some sleep.

"I don't think we should stay here tonight, though," Jonathan says quietly. "I called a friend of mine after I put Seven down. He said I could stay at his vacation home as long as I need. Pets are allowed, so that's not an issue. I don't want to stay here tonight and worry that Pavma's not the only soldier who's been sent for Connery. It'll make my good looks wither with stress wrinkles. Can't have that."

I nod. "Thank you. I agree. Even if Pavma says no one is coming for us, the front window is destroyed and there's blood and a body on the front lawn." I hiss at the massive oversight. "There's a body on the front lawn!"

Jonathan holds up his hands. "Bodhi got rid of the body. I didn't ask how, and you don't need to either. It's done."

I lean my forehead to his shoulder, my arms banding around my stomach. "I'm ruining your life."

Of all things, Jonathan chuckles. "It's your turn. I ruined your life in middle school when I accidentally let it slip that you had feelings for Missy Lahmen."

"You didn't mean to, and it's not your fault kids are cruel."

Jonathan rests his chin atop my head. "It's not your fault that murdering psycho soldiers are after your dog."

"I love you, you know."

"You'd better." He ruffles my hair, then turns toward his bedroom. "I'll pack a bag. You pack some food?"

I nod, summoning energy enough to toss the fancy brand-name food Jonathan keeps on hand into grocery bags.

Connery stands beside me, his tail between his legs. *"Are ye okay? Pavma pulled a fair bit of glass from your skin."*

"I'm not sure if I'm okay. This is more than I thought I

was getting myself into." I keep my eyes on the pantry, pulling out anything that looks easy to make.

Connery lays down in submission. *"Do ye regret me?"*

This stills my movements. "Huh?"

"If ye hadn't taken me in, none of this would be happening. My first chance I get to have a life, I ruin someone else's."

I narrow an eye at him. "But if I hadn't taken you in, then I wouldn't be me, and at the end of a long day, I'm glad I can at least say that hasn't been taken away. I always manage to land on my feet." I grimace. "In time, after I get a job somehow with no social security number and no identity and no bank account." I lean my head to the edge of the shelf, pacing myself as the agony of uncertainty washes over me. "I'll figure it out. I didn't know how to be a mom, but I worked out a plan for raising Seven. I'll get us a place to live and get us back on our feet."

"Then what do ye need from me? How can I help?"

I need too much, I want to admit. Instead, I offer a meek, "Kindness. That's all I ever need. It's my job to do the other things for myself."

Connery looks up at me with insecurity plain on his features. *"You'll let me stay with ye when I return, even after all tha's happened because of me being near ye?"*

I gnaw on my lower lip, wondering if I will ever be stern enough to turn out a dog with a brace on his leg. "You can stay as long as you like. I don't want you to leave us. But you're a free man, Connery. You can go wherever you like. I'm not going to make you stay or tell you to leave. You deserve to be able to make your own choices."

Connery exhales, as if I've granted him some big favor. As if this shadow of a life is a thing to be fought for and won.

What a sad existence for both of us.

I kneel and hug Connery without the usual hesitation I get when I'm around people. "I don't like it that you're worried I'll kick you out. I want you with us. But I know you'll need to go back to Crimshade to deliver the medicine to the prisoners. And I'll need to stay here, so I can be a mom." I whisper in his floppy ear, "But after that's all done, will you come back to me?"

Connery nuzzles my cheek. *"I never thought I'd be considered lucky, but if I found favor with ye, then I guess tha's exactly what I am."*

"We're both lucky," I rule. I kiss his maw and then stand, packing more food for the road. I don't want to think about how sad I would be without Connery, but the prospect looms ahead, warning me that the worst is yet to come.

THE SEPARATE ROAD FORWARD

Jonathan and I load up Jonathan's car and mine in silence, feeling the sting that soon we will be saying goodbye to Connery, Pavma, and Bodhi. It's an hour's drive to the vacation home loaned to us by Jonathan's friend. Seven sleeps the entire way in the backseat beside Connery, who watches her like a hawk, making sure her blanket stays tight around her so she doesn't get chilly.

My best friend doesn't say a word about our little group splitting off in the morning, but I can tell by the tightness of his movements as we unpack the cars upon our arrival that he is not looking forward to the goodbye either.

The vacation home is spacious enough for us to all breathe a little, spreading out to choose separate rooms or one of the many sofas that unfold into beds.

I don't ask but simply claim one of the bedrooms for Seven, who is still sleeping, thank goodness. I carry her to the master bedroom with her mouth open and drool leaking out onto my arm.

Gotta love her.

Bodhi is fidgety as he sets the bags of food on the kitchen counter. He stares at the silver faucet on the sink as if it might hold all the secrets of the universe. Now that I have two hands free, I help put away the perishables into the fridge, respecting Bodhi's melancholy for what it is: facing impending doom.

I can feel his emotions acutely, almost as strong as if they were my own. He doesn't want to return to Crimshade, broken as it is. He wants to stay with us, as if the nothing I have to offer is a thing to be coveted or missed. But I know that his duty to his people will take him away in the morning, and I'm not about to stop him from doing the right thing.

I don't speak, nor do I make him talk about it. Pavma and Connery are scouting the grounds to make sure we're safe. Jonathan is on the phone with his friend, thanking him for the rental.

Bodhi turns his head to me, letting me catch the full brunt of his melancholy. He extends his arm out to the side, silently inviting me to tuck into his nook in a half-embrace.

Which is usually a whole lot more than I can handle.

But it's Bodhi, and ever since we were struck by that magical lightning, I don't hesitate so much around him. If he is sad, then I can't dismiss his feelings or shirk away.

Perhaps because there is no one near to witness my moment of growth, my feet move to Bodhi and my arms wrap around him, pulling him to me so I can absorb some of his sadness.

A deep sigh I did not see coming fills us both the moment the contact unites us. I rest my head on his taller shoulder while he presses his cheek to my hair. It's heady, this connection that seems to settle me more than anything I've ever felt before. Though, to be fair, it's a short list of people I snuggle up to.

"This is intoxicating. Dangerous," Bodhi comments, though he doesn't pull away. "I thought it would have faded by now."

"What?"

"The vonding charm to pull energy from you. It should have only lasted half an hour or so, and it should be fading. But it's only growing stronger. Don't you feel it?"

I swallow hard. The childish part of me wants to deny that hugging Bodhi settles me in a way I cannot do for myself. "I feel... calm when you're near. That's not abnormal, right?"

Bodhi kisses the top of my head again. "I feel calmer too. But it's more than that. When I blew out the glass from the window, I only meant to send a gust of wind at the soldiers to knock them over. I didn't realize it would be that powerful. I've never done anything like that before."

I gasp but remain in his arms. "That was you?"

"I'm sorry I frightened you. I know I did. I frightened myself. The closer in proximity the two of us are, the easier it is to access magic I've never been able to touch. It's not hurting you? I would have thought me shattering the windows would have knocked you to your knees, what with how much magic something like that requires."

I lean into his body, gluttonously settling into his warmth. "The only time it was bad was when you used magic while we weren't together. Then I felt sick."

Bodhi nods, calculating this new information. "Then I won't use it when I return to my homeland. It's a moot point, really. Spells like these don't last. The connection will be gone by morning. Odd that it hasn't faded yet."

The thought of losing this source of warmth and comfort causes a wave of distress to wash through me. Though I've lived my whole life without it until just this week, part of me feels irrevocably linked with Bodhi, for better or worse.

I can only hope things don't get terribly worse, though I'm wondering if that's a fool's hope at this point. Crimshade doesn't really seem to have an upside.

"We have no plan," I tell him, worrying aloud. "You need me nearby if you're going to tap into my lifeforce to increase your magic, but won't that make you easier to spot? And if the bond is fading, how are you going to slip in and out of prison cells undetected?"

Bodhi shushes my fretting, though I know my worries are also his own; he just doesn't want to say them aloud. "It's going to be fine, poppet. Only other mages can sense magic used on that level, so I can't imagine they'll be able to detect me porting back to Crimshade, because our vond will be gone by then." He inhales the top of my head. "It won't matter anyway. The link should already be severed. I'm sure it will be gone by morning. I'll find a way to get the medicine into the prisons. Pavma can help. If he can get himself assigned to prison duty, that's our easy in to get the medicine to the prisoners."

I nod into his chest. "Then I shouldn't be worried. I shouldn't be scared that I'll never see you again." Insecurity washes through me. "It's just the vond that's making me feel as if I'm never going to be okay again if you leave. I don't even know you. Not really. It's an artificial closeness that'll fade by morning."

Bodhi's words sound hollow when he replies. "Absolutely. It all gets to be a strange memory that we look back on and one day feel grateful for." He kisses the top of my head yet again, as if he too can't stand even an inch of separation. "I am grateful to have known you, Zara."

Emotion sticks itself in my throat. I don't know how to tell him that I believe in this connection that is clearly a lie, and that I fear the emptiness that will choke the life out of me when he leaves.

Maybe I shouldn't have kept so many people at bay, not letting them close so they didn't have the chance to reject me. "It's not so bad, loving you," I rasp.

Then I separate my body from his before we absorb more connection that will bury itself deep in my psyche, making our separation that much more difficult to bear. I made my peace long ago that people aren't mine to keep. My father split when my mom was pregnant with me. My mother died when I was barely an adult. My sister died when Seven was only four years old.

Jonathan is one of the few constants in my life, along with my daughter. I let myself cling to them, be weak for them, fight for them. Everyone else comes and goes and I barely let myself notice.

But tonight, as I tuck myself in beside Seven and Jonathan in the master bedroom, I notice the impending absence of Bodhi—this man who was a stranger to me one short week ago.

I'm exhausted after insisting that Connery not sleep with me tonight, and watching his tail dip between his legs. It's too difficult to connect my heart to him yet further when we both know he will be gone in a few hours' time. I'd rather break my heart now, rather than wait for morning after another furry nighttime snuggle that I've grown to treasure.

I toss and turn through the night, plagued by the sight of Bodhi, Connery, and Pavma leaving before the sun rises.

Leaving without saying goodbye.

Leaving a note in the mailbox for us.

Leaving with the sacks of medicine to do their duty for their people, and not looking back at the family who loves them as they march to their bloody doom.

MISSING MEN

I wake in a cold sweat, blinking several times before the room comes into focus. It takes me a breath or two before I remember that my dream wasn't real and this home I'm in isn't familiar because I only just got here last night.

I lean back on the pillow, running my hand over my face as the terror of the nightmare leaves me and logic floods in to replace it. What horrors am I afraid of?

The horror of Bodhi not saying goodbye? We sort of did that last night.

The horror of Bodhi leaving? I've only known him a week. The bond is artificial. It's not real. It's a twist of magic that is trying to convince me it's not a fabrication that will fade.

In fact, since it's morning, I'm guessing the bond is

already gone. Perhaps that unsettling dream was the last of the vonding charm leaving my system.

It's just as well. After Connery, Bodhi, and Pavma leave, we can start over. That's how it should be.

I shouldn't have made Connery sleep with the guys. It would have been nice to have one last night of cuddling my favorite dog in the world before he leaves.

But that didn't happen, I remind myself. We can have a nice breakfast together with the eggs I packed. Connery will tell me his brilliant plan that means he found a way to go safely back to his homeland without danger of execution.

My stomach hollows at the idea that Connery will be leaving today. I can't think about it without my entire being hollowing.

But people aren't mine to keep, and neither are animals.

I sit up carefully so as not to wake Jonathan and Seven. Connery didn't sleep with me last night, but when I open the bedroom door, I nearly trip over his furry form.

"Oh! Good morning, sunshine." I try my hand at sweet levity, but I'm still coming out of my anxiety from the restless sleep I endured. "Go back to sleep. I'm going to make breakfast for everyone. Eggs alright?"

Connery leans into my touch when I run my fingers over his head. *I'll eat a squirrel. We need to conserve food.*

I nod, wishing that wasn't true. But he's right. Everything we eat, wear, and do is on Jonathan's dime. I know my bestie would never say anything about that, but I feel the sting of not having a job. I am new to this version of unemployment, and I hate it already.

Connery follows me into the kitchen.

"I've never not had a job," I tell him. "I'll find something once things settle down. Then I won't be dependent on Jonathan." Though, how I'm going to find a job without identification or a bank account is beyond me. And what about Seven? How can I enroll her in school when she doesn't exist anymore?

"I can homeschool Seven," I say quietly to Connery, thinking aloud. "But then I won't be able to work as often because I'll need to be at home with her. Maybe Jonathan can be with her in the evening. I'll homeschool her during the day, and then while she's with Jonathan, I can work in the evening." I take out the eggs and locate a bowl to whisk them with a fork. "I need money so I can get us a place to live. If Jonathan can put the home I find us in his name, I can pay for it but he'll technically own it. There's the workaround for that."

Connery watches me worry aloud as he sits in the corner of the kitchen. *"You're my m'dolla. Ye don't need to worry about any of this. I'll get us a house and anything else ye need. Wherever ye are, there will I be."*

I smirk at his cuteness. "Thanks. But you're not going to be here. Are we not going to talk about the fact that you're leaving with Bodhi and Pavma today once they wake up? Are we living in denial? Because I'm all for that."

Connery fixes me with a serious look that only he can deliver. *"Bodhi and Pavma are gone. They left in the middle of the night after ye went to sleep. You're my m'dolla; I won't leave ye. Besides, I can't return to Crimshade if I want to keep my head."*

I freeze, then race to the guest bedrooms, throwing them open to see if my bad dream wasn't just my imagination turning cruel on me. "What? Bodhi! Pavma! Bodhi?" I run through the house, opening every door I find.

They can't be gone. It can't be real. I wanted to have breakfast with them. I wanted to make sure Bodhi knew he could come back to us once the job of curing people of the traitor's disease was complete.

My steps are slow when I return to the kitchen, uninterested in breakfast now. "They really left?"

Connery lays on the linoleum. *"They wanted to cross over before the sun rose. Best chance of slipping by undetected. The longer Bodhi can remain hidden, the better their chances of curing the people in prison."*

"But the people will still be in prison. Cured but incarcerated," I say slowly. "Do you think your king will let them go free just because they're getting healthier? Because from what you've told me of King Artifice, I'm thinking his compassion doesn't extend past his vanity." I shake my head, silently cussing in anger. "We didn't go over this together. We didn't make a solid plan. Bodhi has no backup other than Pavma, who can't let anyone know he is working with Bodhi. This is a mess, and we let it happen!"

Connery rests his head on the floor. *"It was always going to be a mess. There's no hope for a peaceful ending. The only thing we can do—the point of the medicine—is to give the people hope and perhaps some time to come up with a way to revolt. If the king doesn't set them free, he's going to have a hard time selling it to the people that his word is wise and worth following. A king rises and falls on either the love and loyalty of his people or the cruelty of his army. Artifice gave up on winning over the people long ago. It's time they had hope enough to rise up against him. Tha's what Bodhi's crossing over to give them. Hope."*

"You're playing the long game, then?"

"It's the only game I know." Connery sits up and stretches out his back legs. *"Neither will work—the short game or the long game."*

It's then that something obvious occurs to me. "You didn't go with them."

Connery regards me warily. *"I have nothing to return to. I wanted to help cure the people, but Bodhi wisely pointed out tha if I go back, I die. I don't have the means to make myself invisible to be helpful to the cause. I don't have the influence to persuade the people. I'm hated by both sides. My life in Crimshade is over."* He starts pacing, walking in circles because his worry is starting to take over. *"I thought ye knew tha."*

"We didn't talk about it. The guys left this morning without saying goodbye. We haven't talked about any of this. I thought you were going with them."

"So did they. So did I. But Bodhi's right. The best chance of getting the medicine to the prisoners is if they go in undetected. If I go, I'm sure to be found and the medicine taken before it can do any good." Connery cranes his head in my direction. *"Ye saved my life in more ways than one, Zara, so I'll stay here and protect your household. You're my m'dolla."*

I set down the whisk and bowl, fixing my fists to my hips. "Do you think I know what that means? You keep saying it, but that's not a thing here."

Connery slows his pacing but doesn't stop completely. *"Jays, I've never had to explain it before. I'm not sure I know how."*

"Well, you're stuck here with me now, so get comfortable and start speaking up. A to Z, soup to nuts, walk me through how me taking you in when you were hurt measures out to you regarding me with the reverence of a queen."

I feel silly even comparing myself to royalty, but it's not far off from how he looks at me.

"M'dolla is a shifter word. It means... My role back in Crimshade was... If anyone should take my focus from serving the king, she's my m'dolla. My loyalty is to her first, and the king and the kingdom second."

"How about the king never? He's an ass."

Connery doesn't respond to my sass. *"My m'dolla is protected by those under my authority, which would have been the whole of the army and the people—everyone the king had put under me."* He lowers his head. *"Now that I am nothing and no one, it's hardly the honor it should be. Ye saved my life. I wanted to bestow an honor upon ye, but I have nothing grand to offer. I suppose the title is more of a gesture at this point, but it's no less true in my heart. I am loyal to ye. I will protect ye and your family. Pavma has sworn to serve me, so he prizes your life, too."*

I don't know which way is up anymore, but I can see true hurt when it stares at me with wounded puppy eyes. I abandon breakfast and slide down to the floor, motioning for him to come to me.

Connery and I both sigh contentedly when his head leans into my hand so we can comfort each other through the rocky waves we thought we had under control.

"Well, if we're coming clean about what little we have to offer, it's my turn. You don't want me to be your m'dolla; I can tell you that right now. It's not possible to protect me. I'm in the mess, elbow deep." I kiss the top of his head. "You can stay with me as long as you like. Forever, in fact. But I guarantee you don't want to protect us. The U.S. Constitution isn't a big enough shield for all we're up against."

Connery sits on my left facing me, so we are nearly

nose to nose. *"Jays, Zara. I'm not useless. Ye don't know all I can do, but you'll see. I can protect ye."*

If I could cry about all I've been through, I would, but the hurt is too deep, and tangled with other emotions that I don't want to touch. "You don't understand what you're up against. In your land, leprosy is leprosy. In mine, leprosy is whatever people don't want to empathize with or understand." I swallow hard, hating that the world is convinced it doesn't have room for us. "Seven is transgender. That means she was born as a boy but feels in her heart that she is supposed to be a girl. I can respect that and let her be who she is, but it's a small group who can do that."

Connery tilts his head to the side. "Is it a problem tha she's a girl now?"

Gratitude for his simple sum-up sweeps over me, pushing me forward to close the small gap between us. I wrap my arms around him, holding him tight. "Sometimes I want to shout that in people's faces. Thank you for saying that. Right now, it's a big, scary thing for people to let children be who they are if it doesn't fit into certain small boxes. When she had to switch schools after her mom died, the parents at the new school protested her. Protested a five-year-old. Picket signs and everything. The school didn't know what to do with her. They forced her to use the boy's bathroom, which was so hurtful and confusing to her that she started having accidents at school. For a while, I picked her up at lunch every day so she could come home and use the bathroom. She's had four bladder infections and she's only seven years old. They hate us, Connery. You can't protect us from that." More trauma spills out of me. "I lost any friends I had, except for Jonathan. They thought I was touched in the head, sick for letting Seven make choices about her own identity. People stick threatening notes on my car. Someone even graffitied my front door, calling me a pervert. I've had Child Protective Services called on me twice for letting her wear dresses to school!"

I can't cry. I don't know how to cry about this. Saying the horrors aloud is the most I can do, and even that is a rare thing. I can feel the poison leeching from my soul where it was sent to rot and fester in the dark. There is no safe place to lay these horrors, except with Jonathan, who has his own set of problems, so I don't like to do that unless I'm boiling over.

"Every day, I'm scared, Connery. Scared that someone will take her away from me because I don't know what I'm doing. Scared that they'll force her to be someone she's not, all so they don't have to coexist with a child who marches to the beat of her own drum. I know in my heart I'm doing the right thing by my sister, and by Seven, but some days it feels like Jonathan and I are the only ones who believe that." I pull back, rubbing my palms hard on my thighs to stop them from trembling. "You don't want to attach yourself to me, Connery. I'm a sinking ship. There is no protecting us from them."

Connery regards me as if my confession is the strangest thing he's ever heard. He harrumphs a few times, and I can tell he is choosing his words carefully. *"Maybe protecting ye means being with ye while the world figures out how to leave children who aren't theirs alone."* He licks my cheek, then nuzzles his head to mine. *"You're doing a good job with her. Seven is a perfect little princess. You're my m'dolla, so tha means Seven is under my protection. No one will leave threatening notes on your door if I'm here."*

I close my eyes, letting his words fill me with that dreaded oxygen of hope that portends to fill and then deflate my lungs. "I want you to stay because I'm selfish," I admit. "But if you were smart, you would leave us and start over on your own. I have nothing to offer you. The roof over my head isn't even mine to share. But if you left, I would never recover. I love that you're here. That you're you. See? Selfish."

Connery doesn't talk me out of my funk, nor does he consent to despairing in the pit of depression with me. He only leaves my side to grab a blanket from the couch and drag it over to me, covering my legs so I don't catch a chill on the floor.

"Maybe ye don't need an army," he finally says quietly. Then he rests his paw atop my hand. *"Maybe ye just need someone to stand with ye when it's hard."*

I nod, unsure how he found the perfect words when I handed him a spaghetti mess and basically told him not to try sorting through the madness.

While Connery and I come from two very different worlds with two very different sets of rules and expectations, for this moment, I am grateful we found each other. I'd stopped believing that people could accept us as we are.

I forgot that the world has the ability to be kind.

29

BODHI AND BARF

Talking about some of the things we've gone through is exhausting, and I hate doing it. I'm glad it's over. Now I can sit in the kitchen, petting my dog in silence for a few beats.

But just when I begin to relax beside Connery, an unsettling stirring starts in my stomach. My mouth tastes like rust all of a sudden, and my limbs ache as if they've been bruised.

Bile churns in my gut at an alarming rate. "I don't feel so great. Back up, Connery. I think I'm going to be sick. What the heck?"

I barely make it to my feet before vomit spills out of me. I bend over the kitchen sink while my eyes water. Food I don't even remember eating forces its way up my throat and out of my mouth so violently; I can hardly keep myself upright.

"Connery, go!" I work out between heaves. "I don't want to get you sick."

But I don't think this is a common flu. In fact, the longer I puke, the more I am certain I know what this is.

It's the same feeling I had when Bodhi used his magic when we weren't near each other.

The connection isn't broken. The vonding charm he used hasn't faded, but in fact seems far more potent, so much that when I squinch my eyes shut as the next bout of sick rolls out of me and splashes in the sink, I can clearly see Bodhi and Pavma as if I was right beside them.

"They've crossed over," I work out, then vomit all over again. "They're in Crimshade. It's..." I pause for another wave of sick. "Bodhi has to be invisible. He's tapping into me without realizing it." My knees weaken as I brace myself on the counter.

I faintly hear Connery's angry growl. *"Tapping into ye? What does tha mean?"*

I keel over, my head in the sink. "Jonathan! Get Jonathan!"

I can't stop throwing up. I'm struggling keep myself upright. My entire being is moments away from crumpling if I don't force oxygen into my lungs. I can barely breathe through all the vomit, and there's no end in sight.

Connery barks as he races out of the kitchen, leaving me to choke on the bile that rages out of me. I grip the edge of the sink for dear life, hoping that I can keep my knees from collapsing.

Pressure builds behind my eyes, forcing tears out of me that laid dormant while I was spilling the depths of my frustration with the world to my dog. It feels like the vomit is coming out of my pours, forcing every toxin out of me, along with vital nutrition and hydration.

"Jon-than!" I cry out while the world blurs. My legs are shaking and give out completely when my best friend rounds the corner, his sleepy eyes widening at the sight of me.

"Zara!" He runs around the counter and braces me with his body from behind, holding me upright while my stomach protests my very existence. "What happened? Did you eat something bad?"

I cannot answer him. I can barely keep my thoughts from blurring one into the other.

Bodhi's visage swims in my mind's eye. He is standing to the side of a scrum of soldiers, who are questioning Pavma of all he's seen.

"Dead," Pavma confirms. "Beneen, Bodhi, and Captain Connery. All dead. I barely escaped with my life, but I've returned."

I can tell that Bodhi is invisible because no one is addressing his presence, and he doesn't seem to be in distress, even though there are plenty of soldiers around. He's nervous, though. I can feel him marveling at how seamlessly he is able to remain invisible, how little effort it's costing him.

Because he's pulling from my lifeforce without realizing it.

"Pavma is being welcomed back," I tell Jonathan and Connery between gasps. "That's a good thing. They aren't interrogating him, but more getting the scoop."

Several soldiers bow their heads, their expressions tight at the confirmation of Connery's death. "Then it's done." They don't seem dismayed or pleased at the news.

One of the sneering soldiers has a shaved head, his pale complexion the brightest thing in the forest. He spits on the ground. "We have nothing to fear because we are not traitors, like that dog. Connery deserves the death he got. I can only hope his ending was long and painful. Being shoved to the top of our ranks all because Highbron could control his every move was a slap in the face to all of us who fought our way up the old-fashioned way."

Pavma doesn't lean into the bitterness. Instead, he holds himself straighter. "I should hope none of us rejoices in the downfall of our captain. These are dour times, indeed."

The chatter fades as Bodhi steps back with several large garbage bags filled with the medications looped over his arms. He moves quietly to make sure his presence is not detected.

When a man marches toward them, the soldiers stand at attention, turning to the newcomer who looks like a professional wrestler. "Officer Pavma. What news have you from Common?"

Pavma relays the same line of lies as seamlessly as he did the first time. He tells the newcomer that Connery, Bodhi, and Beneen died, but he escaped with his life. Pavma inclines his head to the beefy man. "The army is yours, Captain Wash."

Captain Wash doesn't look pleased or put out by this knowledge. If he feels anything at all, he does not show it. "Very good. Back to your post, then."

Pavma lowers his head. "Yes, sir." But when Pavma walks, he does so with an exaggerated limp.

Pavma wasn't injured when he left us. Why is he limping?

I can feel Bodhi's silent urging, as if I am hearing his thoughts via a whisper in my mind. *"Don't overdo it. Wash has a keen eye."*

"Officer Pavma, you were injured?" the new captain asks in that same unfeeling way.

"Yes, sir. It was a long fight to take the former captain down."

Captain Wash motions to the opposite direction. "You're not ready for your normal post, then. See what you can do for the prison guards. There are long bouts where you can sit down until you're back on your feet."

"Yes, Captain."

"Pavma looks too happy," Bodhi says to himself. As clearly as if Bodhi was beside me, I can hear his unspoken voice, just as I can when Connery speaks.

While I am glad that their plan is heading in the right

direction, I know that if they don't get the medicine to the prisoners soon, Pavma is going to be on his own because Bodhi will have lost the ability to tap into my lifeforce.

Which should have happened already.

Jonathan is shouting something, but I can't understand him.

I'm fading. I can feel myself reaching the end of my rope.

"Mommy!" Seven screams.

Just when I didn't think it could get any worse, my baby girl sees me heaving and sweaty, with puke on my chin and my eyelids drooping.

Jonathan holds me up, shouting for Connery to get Seven back into her bedroom.

I can't stop throwing up.

I also can't breathe. The vomit is coming so hard and fast that oxygen is an afterthought.

Both worlds begin to blur—both mine and Bodhi's.

The last thing I see is Connery herding Seven back down the hall, smeared with a colliding vision of the soldiers, whose eyes lock in on Bodhi.

He gasps, realizing that he is no longer invisible.

Only our connection hasn't broken because I can still feel his jolt of fear. It's not that the charm has ended, but instead that I have reached the end of my lifeforce. Bodhi has drained it all, and now he doesn't have the magic available to keep himself invisible.

I scream when they charge at Bodhi, knocking him to

the ground and binding his hands behind his back, pressing his face to the forest floor. The huge black garbage bags filled with the medicine are ripped from him, along with the hope of the prisoners being cured.

The vomit finally stops and both worlds come to a crashing halt, fading from my vision as I collapse in Jonathan's arms.

30

THE NEW PLAN

have no idea what day, time, or month it is when I finally open my eyes.

"Quiet, Sev. Here, let's go play outside. Give Mommy some more time to rest."

"She's dead," Seven says, completely flat. "I don't know why you think I don't know things. I know what dead looks like. My first mom is dead, and now my second mom. Just say it."

That's not my little girl. My baby is joyful and full of optimism.

I feel Jonathan's fingers on my wrist. "Nope. You and I don't lie to each other, remember? I would tell you if she was dead. I can feel her pulse. Come here. See?"

Tiny fingers hold my wrist, and immediately, my heart jerks in my chest, giving me the fortitude to open my eyes.

"Baby?" I croak.

Jonathan swears while Seven throws her body over mine. For several minutes, there is a tornado of movement in the vacation home. A cup of water is tipped to my lips. A blanket is straightened over my supine form. I'm on a leather couch with a large empty plastic container beside me, I'm guessing in case I barf again.

Connery licks my fingers over and over, while Seven presses her cheek to my stomach.

She's scared. I scared her.

"I'm so sorry," I rasp. "I didn't mean for you to see me like that."

Seven squeezes my frame that feels hollow and sore. "You can't do that! You can't die! I need you!"

If she keeps up with this, I'm going to cry, and I'm not sure that would be the best use of what little hydration I've managed to conserve.

Jonathan props me up with several pillows that I hope I don't barf all over. "Why didn't you tell me you were sick? The hiding thing doesn't work for us. If you're sick, you tell me. That's how we work. Your pride pisses me off, and you know it."

I shake my head. "I'm not sick."

Jonathan's nostrils flare, but to his credit, he keeps his tone level. "Sev, I need a minute to talk to your mom. Can you watch TV in my room for one whole show, and then she's all yours?"

Seven kisses my cheek. "You smell horrible, but I still love you." Then she reluctantly parts from my side, kissing

Connery atop his head before moving into the master bedroom to have full control of the remote.

Jonathan waits until he hears the click of the door shutting before he unleashes. "Do not lie to my face, telling me you're not sick. You passed out in my arms! That's not a normal flu. What aren't you telling me? Don't you know that we can't keep secrets from each other?"

I scared him. I really scared him. So often I focus on how alone I am that it doesn't dawn on me that Jonathan is just as isolated at times. He has a social life, but not so much a personal one, aside from Seven and me.

It's an effort to reach out and touch his cheek, but I manage to make it, trusting his hand will hold mine in place. "I would never do that to you. I'm not sick. Not really. It's Bodhi."

Connery straightens, letting out an animated snort.

Jonathan's mouth firms. "What are you talking about?"

I take a deep breath before I unroll the story I barely understand myself. "When we stole the medication that last time, it wasn't possible for Bodhi to get us in and out without him passing out all over again. So, I let him tap into me."

Jonathan's tone turns grave. "You did what?"

I refuse to shrink under the weight of his disapproval, or the menace of Connery's low growl. "It was the only way to get us in and out safely. Bodhi did this spell where he connected us—tethered us together. He needed to tap into my lifeforce so he could access a more powerful magic that he can't reach on his own. It's called a vonding charm. It worked just fine. The only problem is that it was supposed to wear off by now, but I don't think it has. I saw…"

I gasp as snippets of memory come back to me. "When I fainted, Bodhi couldn't draw from me anymore. He's not invisible! The soldiers saw him! They handcuffed him and took the medicine! Bodhi's in trouble!"

Jonathan rears back. "You can't know that."

I try to grip Jonathan's shirt, but my fingers have no dexterity. "Jonathan, I saw Bodhi! I could feel his fear. It's because I fainted that he was found!" I close my eyes in agony. "All that work for nothing! Captain Wash seized the medicine. They have Bodhi!"

Connery backs away from me, breathing in heavy snorts through his nose. *"How did ye know tha name? And it's Officer Wash, not Captain."*

"I saw the whole thing! Wash was promoted to your position, Connery, so now he's the captain of the king's army. I saw everything as if I was right beside Bodhi because he was tapping into me. Only I don't think he knew he was doing it."

Connery is livid with me, pawing at the floor. *"Ye tethered your lifeforce to Bodhi? Didn't I tell ye how dangerous tha would be?"* He shakes his head with a swift snort. *"It don't matter. The connection doesn't last more than a few hours in the rare occasions tha it actually works. Still, it was a bad idea,*

Zara. Ye never should've agreed to the vonding charm. I told Bodhi not to try tha."

"It lasted all night." I tap my chest with a feeble finger. "I can still feel Bodhi's fear. We're tied."

Jonathan starts breathing heavily. "If that's true and he taps into you again, you won't make it. Zara, I'm surprised you're alive."

Connery paces the living room. "*Zara is breathing because Bodhi is still alive. He draws from her, but he needs her heart beating if he's to use the connection. The connection won't let her die so long as it's intact. But it's never lasted this long before. Never in history. Most of the times I've read about, it's only lasted a handful of minutes. A few hours at most. But ye can still feel him?*"

I nod. "I can't see through his eyes right now, but I can feel him. We have to help Bodhi. He's been captured."

Jonathan's voice is grave. "If they're linked and they execute Bodhi for going rogue, what will that do to Zara?"

Connery opens his maw but doesn't answer.

My hand cups my throat as dread rises in me. I can hear the words Connery will not say.

If they kill Bodhi for ditching his tracking anklet while he was supposed to be finding Connery, then my life will be forfeit, too.

I cannot allow that. I don't even care about my own mortality for my sake. If I die, there will be no mother to take care of Seven. She needs me to be alive. She needs me to take care of her.

I try to sit up, but Jonathan has to help me. "We have to get Bodhi out of there. If he dies while we're connected... I can't leave Seven without a parent."

Jonathan holds me to his chest, leaning over so I don't sway. "She's mine, too. You aren't alone in this."

My eyes squinch shut in agony. "We have to break Bodhi out of captivity. I need to get him out of there."

Connery whines. *"The connection should have already faded. Maybe if we wait a little longer, it will break on its own."*

My volume peaks. "And what then? We just leave Bodhi to rot in jail? That wasn't the plan!"

"T'was the inevitability he knew might happen," Connery reminds me. *"None of us expected to live this long once the disease took us. We're both living on borrowed time, willing to cause as much chaos as we can before we're snuffed out."*

Anger floods my weakened system. "Then we'll do exactly that."

I realize that I am talking as if Bodhi and I are the same person. I know I have gone over the deep end.

I also don't care.

"I'm not going to leave Bodhi to rot," Connery explains. *"I'm going back there while ye wait here for me. I'll either come back with Bodhi, or not at all."*

I pinch the bridge of my nose. "You know you can't go back to Crimshade, Connery. The king wants you dead. Besides, I can see through Bodhi's eyes. I can find him once he wakes. I'll go to him, somehow bust him out of jail, he'll sever the bond, and that's that."

Connery shakes his head. "*Ye don't know the first thing about getting around in my world.*"

"Then I'll learn on the fly."

Jonathan leans back after he props me up on the pillows. "Getting Bodhi out is the right thing to do, but there's no way we can bring Seven over into Crimshade. It's too dangerous."

I look up at him, a silent plan forming between us as if we share one messy brain.

Jonathan swallows hard. "I'll stay behind with Seven. If anything should happen to you, you can trust me to raise her."

I reach out and hold his hand as best I can. "If I don't go and sever this connection, I won't be of much use to either of you."

Jonathan kisses my forehead. "I know." He turns his head to my dog. "Connery, you can take her to the prison? You can get her there so she and Bodhi can break the tie, and you can get Bodhi out of there?"

Connery lowers his head. "*I know the way, but I cannot guarantee her safe return. But with my life, I will protect her.*"

Danger rattles in my veins, alerting me to the fact that I am about to do something I will regret for the rest of my life.

But if I don't go, then an entire world will be sentenced to suffer under the thumb of a very curable disease.

If I don't find Bodhi, I might be tethered to him forever,

losing all ability to truly be there for Seven when she needs an alert, functioning parent.

I regret my choice already, but I know that this is the only way forward. I will find Bodhi and get him out of jail. Once our connection is severed, I will come back home to the family who deserves to have me at my best, but still loves me even though I might never be enough.

I will not take them for granted but will do whatever it takes to return to them without fear of separation ever again.

The end.

Love the book?
Leave a review.
Otherwise, I will cheerfully kill Bodhi.

31

SELFISH GIRL

Enjoy a free preview of Selfish Girl, book two in the Crimshade Chronicles.

Selfish Girl

I'm not sure how I got into this mess, but I am inclined to blame the dog.

It's one thing to help a stray get back on his feet. But that was where my good deed was supposed to have ended. I don't want to be filling a backpack for a trip to a land that sounds more fictional than I can stomach, with more danger than I am prepared to face on my own.

A fairytale has basically come to life right before my eyes, but the whole thing is wasted on someone as jaded and weighted as me.

I would have loved this sort of thing in my teen years. As it is now, I'm just worried.

Connery moves his head under my palm, reminding me that I won't be alone on this trek. I'll have my new dog...

...who is actually a huge wolf-bear-dog. Well, technically, I suppose Connery is some sort of shunned right hand to the king of a strange and crappy land called Crimshade. He's a shifter. The last one in Crimshade.

The moment Connery reached adulthood, he lost his free will, being bound to blindly serve King Artifice and his mage Highbron. Connery only recently got his will back when he came down with the dreaded disease that's been thought to be brought on by disloyalty to the throne (which shouldn't have been possible, since Connery's ability to think and act for himself was stripped away by Highbron).

But to me, Connery is the dog I always wanted. I can hug him whenever I want and tell him things I'm too embarrassed to admit aloud to my best friend.

Which isn't a long list, since Jonathan and I are freakishly and probably unhealthily joined at the hip.

Except for today, because I've left my adopted daughter (who is also my niece) with Jonathan, so I can cross over into Crimshade to help save a people I have no attachment to or affinity for.

Still, it seems like the right thing to do—bringing them medicine to treat their leprosy, which is curable by our standards, but beyond what their medicine understands.

Mostly I'm going to Crimshade to find Bodhi, who was captured by the king's soldiers and locked away.

Bodhi.

My stomach is in knots, thinking about the friend I never saw coming, and the bond that hasn't faded. The vonding charm Bodhi performed was supposed to temporarily link us so he could tap into my lifeforce to increase his dwindling magic.

The key word is "temporarily". But instead of fading, the bond seems to be strengthening, which isn't how this sort of thing goes, as I understand it. When Bodhi was captured, I saw the whole thing through his eyes. When he used more of his magic while tapping into me, it made me so sick that I passed out after barfing up what I'm sure was the entire weeks' worth of food. That sort of thing doesn't happen when we're in close proximity to each other, but being that Bodhi is in an entirely other world, it's problematic for us to be vonded while we're so far apart.

More than wanting to relieve the physical discomfort, the vonding charm gave me a soft spot for Bodhi. It's like I understand him now, even though we've only known each other a week. He's important to me.

I need to bust Bodhi out of that prison, but I have no idea how.

"I'm scared," I admit in a whisper to Connery. "If anything happens to me, Seven will not be okay. I'm her advocate. I'm her friend. I'm her..." I swallow hard, wishing there was any other way to solve this problem. "I'm her mom."

Connery's head moves to my stomach because he's just that tall. His grayish-brown fur is thick and soft, begging me to stroke it because that is the thing that calms me quickest. His bright blue eyes are filled with wisdom and empathy, and when he looks up at me in the way he is doing now, my insides start to quake. All the insecurities I keep at bay threaten to come tumbling out at his feet.

When he speaks, his maw doesn't move. He communicates as clearly as if he was a person standing right in front of me, his Irish brogue sinking into my mind. *"On my life, I will see ye returned to your daughter."*

Warmth spreads through my chest. When my nephew turned into my niece, and then after my sister's death became my daughter, I didn't realize how little room there is in the world for a transgender child. Getting people to use the correct pronouns and let her use the freaking bathroom is a daily battle I will not leave a seven-year-old to fight on her own.

She has Jonathan, who is no stranger to bigotry. She'll be okay while I'm away.

I hope.

I used to be a little more social. I had a few friends in college. But the world turns on you when you let your child be themselves in a way that people are not ready to accept. Now I walk with my hood over my hair, hands in my pockets as if my black hoodie is actual armor. I don't want people to talk to me or even look my way, because I'm up to my ears in other people's opinions on how I should raise a child that is not theirs.

Connery keeps his head tight to my side as I kneel next to my backpack, shoving a spare change of clothes inside. *"If there was any other way to sever the bond between ye and Bodhi, I would do it for ye so ye didn't have to cross over to Crimshade. The vonding charm he used to connect ye to him should have faded an hour or so after he performed the magic, which he never should have attempted in the first place."* Connery's eyes narrow as he lifts his head to look me in the eye. *"It makes no sense tha he can still draw on your lifeforce to enhance his magic."*

My stomach rumbles. "What makes no sense is me leaving my daughter and Jonathan here. They need me, Connery. And I need them. Most days, they are the only people in my world."

"Now ye have me. Wherever ye are, there will I be." It's a vow I can tell he doesn't take lightly. A vow I want to warn him away from making, though it's already done in his mind. I don't know how to explain to him that I am a sinking ship.

Connery leaves my side only to move to the kitchen in

the vacation home we borrowed from one of Jonathan's friends. He comes back with a banana in his maw, which he nuzzles into my hand.

I peel it for him. "Are you hungry? Here, baby."

Yes, he is a grown man beneath this fur, but I can't always remember that. Most days, he's my precious dog, whom I get to coddle to my heart's content.

Connery tilts his head at me as if I've said something funny. *"No, you're hungry, lass. Your stomach was growling."*

I grimace at the thoughtfulness on his part and the thoughtlessness on mine. I didn't even realize my stomach had rumbled. I'm not used to someone being that attentive to my nuances. "I'm not sure this will stay down. When Bodhi used his magic last, I threw up so hard, I passed out, if you recall. I'm nervous to eat anything, to be honest. Whenever Bodhi uses his magic, he accidentally draws on my lifeforce without meaning to. I'm kind of tired of barfing. I'd rather be hungry."

I can tell this worries Connery just as much as it concerns me. Bodhi doesn't know that he and I are still connected, nor is he the kind of jackweasel who would use his magic if he knew it was physically hurting me when he did so. Bodhi is a good person.

And good people shouldn't be in jail.

That's yet another reason why we need to go to Crimshade to remedy this problem.

Should be simple. Should be quick.

At least, that's what I tell myself when I am faced with saying goodbye to the only people in my life.

Connery stares me down until I eat the entire banana, which earns him a kiss on the snout for being such a precious mother hen.

Since the Crimshade crew barreled into my life, I don't just have Jonathan in my corner; Connery and Bodhi sneaked their way into my heart, filling me with acceptance and kindness I didn't realize I needed from more than just Jonathan.

I zip up my black hoodie. "Where is the portal or whatever to take us to your world? How does it work?"

Connery doesn't answer right away, except with a firm, *"We should go. Ye said your goodbyes to Seven and Jonathan. They left so we could pack and be on our way."*

I swallow hard, knowing that Seven did not fully understand that my absence might be more than a few hours. "I'm ready."

I'm sure it's clear from my shaky tone that I might never be ready to leave the only family I have. They need me.

I straighten, putting aside the worry that's plagued me since we decided this was the way to go. Seven needs me to be alive, so I have to do this. I have to go to Crimshade and sever the vonding charm, or I'll starve faster than I can shove food in my mouth if Bodhi keeps using his enhanced magic.

Connery leads the way out of the house. We don't get

in my car, so perhaps this portal is within walking distance.

"*We need a body of water,*" he informs me.

"How big a body? I don't think we're near any lakes."

Connery sniffs the ground. "*It could be as small as your bathtub, but it has to be naturally flowing water.*"

I point toward the ditch on the side of the road up ahead. "Bigger than that, I'm guessing."

Connery picks up his pace. "*Tha'll do.*"

The ditch is muddy and filled with several fast-food wrappers. Not exactly what I imagined the portal to a magical land should be. Hopefully we just have to stand near it and whisper some odd chant.

Of course it's not that simple.

Connery holds no hesitation as he stomps right into the muck, turning to look up at me expectantly. "*This way.*"

I frown. "I was hoping not to be soggy and muddy when I crossed over."

Connery sees my hesitation for the disgust it is. I swear, he smirks at me. I'm not sure how he manages the twinge of a facial expression as a dog, but I see his amusement plain on his furry face. He moves to my side and licks my hand. "*This is the way. If I was a mage, I could port into Crimshade from anywhere. But as I'm not, this is how we get there.*"

My shoulders lower as I gather up my gumption and take the first step forward. I can feel the cold water seeping into my black sneakers, muddying my socks, and making me chilly all over. "Awesome," I drone.

Connery snickers airily as he dips his face into the gross water and begins a chant that is too complicated for me to repeat. He pauses only to stare at me expectantly, waiting until I splash the disgusting water on my face, as well.

I hate this new world already.

I cringe with a sour expression as Connery continues the chant, clearly amused at my revulsion.

I'm about to say something acerbic, but the water begins to glisten with a sheen of lavender over the surface, stilling my protest. "Oh, wow! Connery, it's doing it!"

Connery looks at me questioningly, as if to ask what it is that I expected might happen.

The water turns from a muddy, polluted mess to a glittering lavender glow, tempting me to take a bath in it so my whole body can radiate with this otherworldly shimmer. Though the drainage ditch only holds about six inches of water, suddenly the ground lowers, forcing the water to climb my legs, and then my waist.

"Connery?" I call out shakily, wondering when the water will stop rising, or the ground will stop lowering.

I realize it's the ground that's lowering because the water doesn't overflow onto the main road.

It dawns on me in a wash of panic that I am putting all my trust in a dog, whom I have known for only one week.

Connery stands on his hind legs, gently placing his

paws on either of my shoulders. He is taller than me like this. His expression is that of an elementary school teacher calmly explaining what a fire drill is, and that there's no need to panic.

Fear rushes through me when the water climbs to my chest. "Connery?"

He remains calm, telling me with his beautiful blue eyes that this is all quite normal. *"The water is going to close over your head, but it'll only be for a few seconds. When ye open your eyes again, we'll be in my world."*

I don't care if he knows how scared I am, which is normally something I try to conceal from everyone. I wrap my arms around his torso and rest my cheek on his shoulder. I bury my face in his fur, hoping it will shield me from all that threatens to haunt me and shorten my life.

When the water closes over my head, I shiver against Connery. The water is cold, yes, but it's the fear of the unknown that chills my spine.

One second. Two. Three. Four.

The seconds tick by, but the water does not recede. I should have asked more questions. Any questions, really. I should have told Connery that I'm not a strong swimmer. I don't know how to hold my breath for a long period of time.

My lungs start to ache with the insistence of a child asking for just one more piece of candy.

I clutch tighter to Connery, whose voice is calm when I start to panic. *"We're nearly there."*

I have no idea what to expect when we cross over. I should have studied this new world before agreeing to cross into it. This isn't me. I'm the researcher. I dig into the facts until I am satisfied that I could draw a roadmap blindfolded.

But I trust Connery, even though I'm not sure such a gift is warranted. I barely know him.

Yet I've left Seven alone with him.

Yet he sleeps beside me at night.

Yet here I am, taking his word that he didn't bring me here to let me drown.

I used to be smarter than this.

The moment I debate swimming to the surface, the water breaks over my head. Either it is receding, or the ground is lifting, bringing me into a world where the only person I know is a dog who is supposed to be dead.

I blink the water from my eyes and take in a sight so strange; my first breath is a gasp.

Read *Selfish Girl* by Mary E. Twomey today!

ABOUT THE AUTHOR

USA Today bestselling author Mary E. Twomey lives in Michigan with her three adorable children. She enjoys reading, writing, vegetarian cooking, and telling her children fantastic stories about wombats.

While she loves writing fantasy, dystopian, and paranormal tales for her readers, Mary also writes romance under the name Tuesday Embers, and cozy mysteries under the name Molly Maple.

Visit her online at www.maryetwomey.com, and sign up for her newsletter, so you never miss a new release.

9 781088 177242